序 言

「研究所必考 1000 字」是專爲報考研究所的同學所編輯的。爲了幫助同學在短期內精通研究所字彙,我們特別收集各校研究所歷屆英文試題,電腦統計,整理出**最常考的 1000 個單字**,再搭配試題原本例句,加深印象,方便同學記憶。

本書字彙按照字母序排列,同時,爲了幫助讀者理解字義,書中部分單字也加注字根字首分析,如 collaborate:

$$
\begin{array}{ccc}
\text{col} & + & \text{laborate} \\
| & & | \\
together & + & work
\end{array}
$$

(col + laborate = together + work),「一起工作」即爲「合作」,如此一來,簡單易背。

部分單字也補充同義字，方便同學比較，加強記憶。次外，書中每隔六頁即附有 **Check List**，可供同學做自我評量、驗收學習成果之用。

　　本書能順利完成，除了要感謝外籍老師 Laura E. Stewart 及謝靜芳老師的仔細校對，還要感謝黃淑貞小姐負責設計內文版面，白雪嬌小姐負責設計封面，以及王淑平小姐協助打字，林銀姿老師協助完稿。

　　本書雖經審慎校對，力求正確無誤，但仍恐有疏漏之處，誠盼各界先進不吝批評指正。

編者　謹識

怎樣背完這本單字書

1. 背單字要分音節背，23813148，這個數字如果分為 2-381-3148 就容易背了，因為人類的短暫記憶有限。背英文單字也是一樣，一定要唸出來，分成音節背，才容易記。

2. 單字要大量地背，一天背 5 個，一年不等於 5×365，因為背了後面，會忘了前面，一天如果背 60 個，即使忘了一半，還有 30 個。

3. 將不會背的單字，做一記號，複習起來就快很多，不要重複複習已會的單字。愈記不下來的單字，愈要想辦法記住。不可以勉強死背。

4. 利用已會的單字，和不會的單字加以比較。如 rival（對手）背不下來，就用 arrival（到達）加以比較，將永遠不會忘記。

5. **背不起來的單字**，可以查閱「學習出版公司」出版的「**英文字根字典**」，了解單字原始的意義。

6. 背單字是毅力的考驗，也是記憶力的訓練，每天嘴裡不停地背，你將沒有煩惱，精神很愉快，你會變得更漂亮、更英俊，甚至眼睛發亮，因為你有了目標，未來充滿希望。

7. 背單字剛開始的時候很慢，一但抓到訣竅，就**愈背愈快**，自己給自己計算時間，看背的速度，有沒有進步。

A

absorb 〔əb'sɔrb〕 v. 吸收

There are clearly more people wishing to
immigrate than our society can *absorb*. (84 政大)

abuse 〔ə'bjus〕 n. 虐待

We need to protect our minors in order to
prevent any child *abuse* from taking place.

(88 銘傳)

accede 〔æk'sid〕 v. 同意

We need further information before we
can *accede* to your request.

(90 世新)

ac +	cede
to +	go

accelerate 〔æk'sɛlə,ret〕 v. 加速

The new operating system *accelerates* the
computer's boot-up procedure. (87 中興)

ac +	celer +	ate
to +	swift +	v.

accentuate 〔 æk'sɛntʃʊˌet 〕 *v.* 加重；強調

Tight-fitting jeans that *accentuate* a thin, youthful appearance are in fashion today.

（83 清大）

access 〔'æksɛs 〕 *n.* 使用權

The suspect claimed that he had not been allowed *access* to a lawyer after he was arrested. （87 台大）

accessible 〔 æk'sɛsəbḷ 〕 *adj.* 易接近的；可達到的（= *approachable* ）

Modification of the environment can make it more *accessible* to people with physical disabilities. （87 中正）

accident 〔'æksədənt 〕 *n.* 意外

I saw a nasty *accident* between two cars this morning. （90 彰師大）

accommodate 〔 əˈkɑməˌdet 〕 v. 使適應；容納

Some find it hard to *accommodate* themselves to the new working conditions. (91 世新)

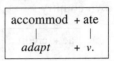

New hotels are being built to *accommodate* the increasing number of visitors. (81 交大)

accomplish 〔 əˈkɑmplɪʃ 〕 v. 完成

The United States Senate *accomplishes* much of its work by means of committees. (86 中興)

account 〔 əˈkaʊnt 〕 n. 原因；說明

The senator declined to give a speech on *account* of a sore throat. (87 台大)

Li Po gave a wonderful *account* of the marvels of the Yellow River in his poem. (84 中興)

accredit 〔 ə'krɛdɪt 〕 v. 任命 (= *appoint*)

When diplomats are *accredited* to a foreign
country, they are representatives of their
own country. (90 交大)

ac + credit	ac + cumulate
| |	| |
to + believe	*to + heap up*

accumulate 〔 ə'kjumjə,let 〕 v. 堆積

After waste material is *accumulated*, it
must be disposed of properly. (84 中山)

accustomed 〔 ə'kʌstəmd 〕 *adj.* 習慣的

I have lived near the railway for so long now
that I've grown *accustomed* to the noise. (86 台大)

acquire 〔 ə'kwaɪr 〕 v. 獲得

I used to dislike cheese, but I *acquired* a
taste for it when I was in
college. (83 中興)

ac + quire
| |
to + seek

acquisition 〔͵ækwə'zɪʃən〕 *n.* 添加物

The museum made an important *acquisition* when it bought the famous painting. (91 清大)

actualize 〔'æktʃuəl͵aɪz〕 *v.* 實現

Our highest human need is to *actualize* ourselves, to become all that we might be.

(86 交大)

acumen 〔ə'kjumən〕 *n.* 心智敏銳;聰明才智

The sales manager is noted for his business *acumen*. (79 政大)

ad hoc 〔'æd'hɑk〕 *adj.* 特別的

An *ad hoc* committee passed a plan to enhance wildlife conservation in Taiwan. (83 淡江)

adapt 〔ə'dæpt〕 *v.* 適應

The immigrant *adapted* to living in his new country. (83 中興)

addict 〔 ə'dɪkt 〕 *v.* 使上癮

John was *addicted* to heroin all his life; he
could never quit the bad habit. (87 逢甲)

addicted 〔 ə'dɪktɪd 〕 *adj.* 上癮的

People can be *addicted* to many things:
drugs, alcohol, TV, etc. (81 交大)

addictive 〔 ə'dɪktɪv 〕 *adj.* 會使人上癮的

Experts claim that jogging is *addictive*; once
you begin to jog, you may be unable to stop.

(88 台大)

adequate 〔'ædəkwɪt 〕 *adj.* 適當的；足夠的

Music expresses a state of meaning for
which there may be no *adequate* word in
any language. (81 交大)

Transportation systems were not *adequate* to
deliver the supplies to remote areas. (81 逢甲)

Check List

( ) 1. accede   A. cause

( ) 2. accentuate   B. hooked

( ) 3. accessible   C. license

( ) 4. accommodate   D. adjust

( ) 5. accomplish   E. assent

( ) 6. account   F. perspicuity

( ) 7. accredit   G. cumulate

( ) 8. accumulate   H. reify

( ) 9. acquisition   I. stress

( ) 10. actualize   J. suitable

( ) 11. acumen   K. available

( ) 12. ad hoc   L. purchase

( ) 13. adapt   M. billet

( ) 14. addicted   N. particular

( ) 15. adequate   O. attain

Vocabulary Ratings

5–7 *Good*   8–11 *Very Good*   12–15 *Excellent*

Synonyms

1. accede
   = assent

2. accentuate
   = stress

3. accessible
   = available

4. accommodate
   = put up

5. accomplish
   = attain

6. account
   = cause
   = grounds

7. accredit
   = license

8. addicted to
   = hooked on

9. acquisition
   = purchase

10. actualize
    = realize
    = objectify

11. acumen
    = perspicuity
    = insight

12. ad hoc
    = particular

13. adapt
    = adjust

14. accumulate
    = amass
    = gather

15. adequate
    = ample
    = suitable

adjacent ﹝ ə'dʒesn̩t ﹞ *adj.* 毗連的

The football stadium is *adjacent* to the
gymnasium. (86交大)

ad +	jac	+ ent
to +	throw +	adj.

administration ﹝ əd,mɪnɪs'treʃən ﹞ *n.* 行政

Public *administration* must be responsible to
the requirements of the people. (89成大)

admit ﹝ əd'mɪt ﹞ *v.* 准許進入

Fifty percent of the applicants were *admitted*
to the program. (81淡江)

adolescence ﹝ ,ædl̩'ɛsn̩s ﹞ *n.* 青春期

The crisis of *adolescence* had brought on an
outburst against parental authority. (80中興)

adopt ﹝ ə'dɑpt ﹞ *v.* 領養；採用

The childless couple decided to *adopt* an
orphaned baby. (85交大)

adversary 〔 ˈædvɚˌsɛrɪ 〕 *n.* 對手；仇敵

(= *opponent*)

Nature is often seen as an *adversary* when disasters occur. (87 政大)

adverse 〔 ədˈvɝs 〕 *adj.* 不利的

(= *unfavorable*)

After the play received *adverse* criticism, few people went to see it. (90 台北)

advise 〔 ədˈvaɪz 〕 *v.* 建議

Beginners are well *advised* to take an easy course. (90 彰師大)

advocate 〔 ˈædvəˌket 〕 *v.* 主張

The writer *advocates* for abused children and spouses. (91 世新)

ad	+ voc	+ ate
to	+ call	+ v.

affability 〔͵æfəˈbɪlətɪ 〕 *n.* 和藹可親；友善

His rare *affability* and sweetness of manner lift the saddest spirits. (80 中興)

affair 〔 əˈfɛr 〕 *n.* 事務

All of us should be concerned with public *affairs* to make our society a better place.

（90 彰師大）

affect 〔 əˈfɛkt 〕 *v.* 影響

The power outage *affected* thousands of people, forcing them to live in the dark. (90 輔大)

affluent 〔ˈæflʊənt 〕 *adj.* 富裕的

No matter how *affluent* our society becomes, we will still have to work. (91 清大)

afford 〔 əˈfɔrd 〕 *v.* 負擔得起

I'm not rich and can't *afford* a new car every year. (81 中山)

aggravate 〔'ægrə,vet〕 v. 加重；惡化

The singer's illness was *aggravated* by the sudden change of temperature early this morning. (84 中興)

ag + grav + ate
to + *heavy* + *v.*

aggressive 〔ə'grɛsɪv〕 adj. 有攻擊性的

The lion is an *aggressive* animal that actively seeks out its prey. (82 台大)

agrarian 〔ə'grɛrɪən〕 adj. 農業的
(= *agricultural*)

The country is primarily *agrarian*; it has developed little industry. (80 淡江)

aim 〔em〕 n. 目標 (= *goal*)

The governor's *aim* is to increase state income. (80 中正)

ajar ﹝ ə'dʒɑr ﹞ *adj.* 半開的

She left the door *ajar* so as to let the cat go in.

(84 政大)

akin ﹝ ə'kɪn ﹞ *adj.* 類似的 (= *similar*)

The two professions are not *akin* in spite of what people commonly think. (82 政大)

alert ﹝ ə'lɝt ﹞ *adj.* 留心的；機警的

Many students drink a lot of coffee to stay *alert* while they are studying. (87 逢甲)

alleviate ﹝ ə'livɪ,et ﹞ *v.* 減輕

Something must be done to *alleviate* the traffic congestion. (83 政大)

allocate ﹝ 'ælə,ket ﹞ *v.* 分配

The charity *allocated* the supplies among the needy people. (85 中興)

al + loc + ate
| | |
to + place + v.

alternative 〔 ɔl'tɜnətɪv 〕 *n.* 另一個選擇

To offset the deficit, the president had no *alternative* but to raise taxes. (81 交大)

ambiguous 〔 æm'bɪgjʊəs 〕 *adj.* 含糊的

It is not clear what the sentence means because it is *ambiguous*. (83 台大)

ambi	+ gu	+ ous
about	+ drive	+ adj.

ambush 〔'æmbʊʃ 〕 *n.* 埋伏

Leftist rebels killed 31 soldiers in an *ambush* on Thursday. (85 清大)

amend 〔 ə'mɛnd 〕 *v.* 修正

There should be a way for individuals to correct or *amend* inaccurate records. (82 交大)

Check List

( ) 1. adjacent
( ) 2. adolescence
( ) 3. adversary
( ) 4. advocate
( ) 5. affability

( ) 6. affluent
( ) 7. aggravate
( ) 8. agrarian
( ) 9. ajar
( ) 10. akin

( ) 11. alleviate
( ) 12. allocate
( ) 13. ambiguous
( ) 14. ambush
( ) 15. amend

A. opponent
B. exacerbate
C. equivocal
D. modify
E. wealthy

F. distribute
G. neighboring
H. snare
I. affiliated
J. promote

K. open
L. puberty
M. relieve
N. cordiality
O. agricultural

Vocabulary Ratings

5–7 *Good*   8–11 *Very Good*   12–15 *Excellent*

Synonyms

1. adjacent
   = neighboring

2. adolescence
   = puberty

3. adversary
   = opponent

4. advocate
   = promote

5. affability
   = cordiality

6. affluent
   = wealthy
   = rich

7. aggravate
   = exacerbate

8. agrarian
   = agricultural

9. ajar
   = open

10. akin
    = affiliated
    = similar

11. alleviate
    = ease
    = relieve

12. allocate
    = distribute

13. ambiguous
    = equivocal

14. ambush
    = snare
    = trap

15. amend
    = modify
    = revise

anarchy 〔'ænəkɪ 〕 *n.* 無政府狀態

The country has been in a state of *anarchy* since the inconclusive election. (91 世新)

an	+ arch +	y
|	|	|
without +	*ruler* +	*n.*

annual 〔'ænjʊəl 〕 *adj.* 一年一次的

We issue an *annual* report every September. (87中正)

ann	+ ual
|	|
year +	*adj.*

anthology 〔 æn'θɑlədʒɪ 〕 *n.* 詩文集

This is an *anthology* of writings by a famous scholar. (81 淡江)

anticipate 〔 æn'tɪsə‚pet 〕 *v.* 預期

The sudden decrease in sales was not *anticipated* by anyone.

(84 中山)

anti	+ cipate
|	|
before +	*take*

antipathy 〔 æn'tɪpəθɪ 〕 *n.* 反感

Don't you think it immoral to declare racial *antipathy* against ethnic minorities? (90 政大)

```
anti  +  path  + y
 |        |      |
against + feelings + n.
```

aphorism 〔'æfə,rɪzəm 〕 *n.* 格言

There is a lot of truth in the *aphorism*, "Morals are caught, not taught." (83 淡江)

appeal 〔 ə'pil 〕 *v.* 吸引

The idea of becoming famous *appeals* to many people. (87 逢甲)

applaud 〔 ə'plɔd 〕 *v.* 鼓掌

At the end of the eloquent speech, the audience *applauded*. (88 世新)

appliance (ə'plaɪəns) *n.* 用具;家電用品

Microwave ovens are among the most common home *appliances*. (88 世新)

aptitude ('æptəˌtjud) *n.* 性向;才能

A language *aptitude* test can determine if you have the ability to learn another language. (90 台大)

ardent ('ɑrdn̩t) *adj.* 熱心的

(= *enthusiastic*)

He has been an *ardent* supporter of Zionism. (85 中興)

ard	+	ent
burn	+	adj.

arduous ('ɑrdʒuəs) *adj.* 困難的

The scientific conquest of fusion energy is proving to be an *arduous* task. (87 中興)

arouse (ə'rauz) *v.* 喚起;激起

Paul's curiosity was *aroused* when he heard a noise outside his bedroom. (80 中山)

arson 〔'ɑrsn̩〕 *n.* 縱火

Peking admitted that the Qiando Lake tragedy was "robbery, murder, and *arson*." (83 淡江)

articulate 〔 ɑr'tɪkjəlɪt 〕 *adj.* (言語) 清楚的

The child was unable to offer an *articulate* description of what she had witnessed. (87 台大)

ascend 〔 ə'sɛnd 〕 *v.* 登上

When King George VI died, his daughter *ascended* the throne. (台大)

a + scend
to + climb

aspect 〔'æspɛkt 〕 *n.* 觀點

Life in its biological *aspects* is an unfathomable secret. (81 交大)

aspiration 〔ˌæspə'reʃən 〕 *n.* 渴望

The government should no longer ignore the political *aspirations* of the local people.

(83 台大)

a + spir + tion
to + breathe + n.

assert 〔ə'sɝt〕 v. 表現自己;聲明

The thief *asserted* his innocence despite the evidence against him.

（86 中興）

```
as+ sert
 |     |
to + join together
```

assertive 〔ə'sɝtɪv〕 adj. 獨斷的

Richard is usually very *assertive* in class.
He has strong opinions about almost every subject. （88 交大）

assess 〔ə'sɛs〕 v. 評估

It's too early to *assess* the effects of the new legislation. （83 淡江）

assets 〔'æsɛts〕 n. pl. 資產

Assets are valuable property and possessions.

（85 銘傳）

assimilation 〔 ə͵sɪml̩'eʃən 〕 *n.* 同化

Becoming a part of America, or *assimilation*, was the goal of most of these immigrants.

（88 交大）

as + simil + ation
| | |
to + *like* + *n.*

<u>sort</u> *n.* 種類
as<u>sort</u> *v.* 分類

assort 〔 ə'sɔrt 〕 *v.* 分類

The goods were *assorted* according to size.

（89 文化）

assortment 〔 ə'sɔrtmənt 〕 *n.* 各種各樣

The population of this area is a *assortment* of people from different ethnic backgrounds.

（84 政大）

astonish 〔 ə'stɑnɪʃ 〕 *v.* 使驚訝

We were *astonished* when we came and found the door open. （90 義守）

Check List

( ) 1. anarchy
( ) 2. anthology
( ) 3. antipathy
( ) 4. aphorism
( ) 5. appliance

( ) 6. aptitude
( ) 7. ardent
( ) 8. arduous
( ) 9. arson
( ) 10. articulate

( ) 11. assert
( ) 12. assess
( ) 13. asset
( ) 14. assimilation
( ) 15. assort

A. zealous
B. propensity
C. evaluate
D. device
E. difficult

F. chaos
G. burning
H. proverb
I. integration
J. collection

K. lucid
L. enmity
M. categorize
N. declare
O. possession

Vocabulary Ratings

5–7 *Good*   8–11 *Very Good*   12–15 *Excellent*

Synonyms

1. anarchy
   = chaos

2. anthology
   = collection

3. antipathy
   = enmity

4. aphorism
   = proverb

5. appliance
   = device

6. aptitude
   = propensity
   = talent

7. ardent
   = zealous

8. arduous
   = difficult

9. arson
   = burning

10. articulate
    = lucid
    = clear

11. assert
    = declare
    = affirm

12. assess
    = evaluate

13. assets
    = possession

14. assimilation
    = integration
    = adaptation

15. assort
    = categorize
    = classify

astronaut 〔'æstrəˌnɔt〕 *n.* 太空人

Have you ever wondered why *astronauts* wear space suits for a "walk" in space? (82 中興)

asylum 〔ə'saɪləm〕 *n.* 庇護；避難所

The Liberian rebels are considering an offer of *asylum* from Nigeria. (85 清大)

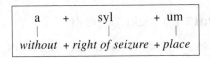

a	+	syl	+ um
without	+	*right of seizure*	+ *place*

attach 〔ə'tætʃ〕 *v.* 認爲有

It is unforgivable that the jury should *attach* no importance to the eyewitness's testimony.

(90 台大)

attain 〔ə'ten〕 *v.* 達到；獲得

Women have not yet been able to *attain* the same economic powers as men. (90 台大)

attend 〔 ə'tɛnd 〕 v. 參加

I was unable to *attend* my niece's wedding because I was sick. (86 台大)

attention 〔 ə'tɛnʃən 〕 n. 注意力

Recent surveys have focused *attention* on the nation's health. (85 台大)

attract 〔 ə'trækt 〕 v. 吸引

This new product has *attracted* a lot of attention. (82 中山)

attribute 〔 ə'trɪbjut 〕 v. 歸因於   *n.* 屬性

People without confidence tend to *attribute* their success to external causes such as luck.

(87 台大)

All living things have certain *attributes* that are passed on from one generation to the next.

(86 中興)

at + tribute
| |
to + bestow

authentic 〔 ɔ'θɛntɪk 〕*adj.* 真實的

I believe the painting is *authentic*, though
some critics still insist that it is an imitation.

（84 台大）

automat 〔'ɔtə,mæt 〕*n.* 使用自動販賣機
販賣食物之餐館

An *automat* is a self-service restaurant where
customers serve themselves. （81 師大）

autonomously 〔 ɔ'tɑnəməslɪ 〕*adv.* 自主地

The departments are not depending on one
another because they operate *autonomously*

（90 政大）

available 〔 ə'veləbḷ 〕*adj.* 可獲得的

According to the latest *available* information,
the air crash took place around midnight.

（87 台大）

avenue 〔'ævə,nju 〕 *n.* 途徑

The agreement between the two countries opened up new *avenues* of trade. (90 輔大)

B

bacteria 〔,bæk'tɪrɪə 〕 *n.pl.* 細菌

Vacuum-packed cans prevent *bacteria* from spoiling the food. (82 中興)

ban 〔 bæn 〕 *v.* 禁止

Last year, many governments *banned* the import of beef from Britain. (86 中興)

bankruptcy 〔 bænk'rʌpsɪ 〕 *n.* 破產

If the manager had planned more carefully, *bankruptcy* might have been avoided. (90 世新)

barricade 〔'bærə,ked 〕 *n.* 路障

People had to park their vehicles far from the schools because of the *barricades*. (89 淡江)

barrier 〔'bærɪə 〕 *n.* 障礙

Humanitarians tried to remove all the *barriers*. (90 義守)

battle 〔'bætḷ 〕 *v.* 奮鬥

The labor union is *battling* for shorter hours, and better medical benefits. (91 清大)

bedridden 〔'bɛd,rɪdn 〕 *adj.* 臥病在床的

While ill with tuberculosis, Jasmine was *bedridden*. (90 中正)

beforehand 〔 bɪ'for,hænd 〕 *adv.* 事前

The man who was seen in the area *beforehand* was the prime suspect in the murder. (88 台大)

behalf 〔 bɪˈhæf 〕 *n.* 代表

In his absence, I would like to thank all
concerned on my brother's *behalf.* (85 台大)

benevolently 〔 bəˈnɛvələntlɪ 〕 *adj.* 仁慈的

That government governs best that governs
most justly and most *benevolently.* (83 中興)

bene	+	vol	+	ent	+	ly
good	+	wish	+	adj.	+	adv.

benign 〔 bɪˈnaɪn 〕 *adj.* 良性的

A *benign* lesion usually
has a regular border.

(90 世新)

beni	+	gn
well	+	produce

beyond 〔 bɪˈjɑnd 〕 *prep.* 超出;非…可及

When I finally got my suitcase back from the
airport, it had been damaged *beyond* repair.

(85 台大)

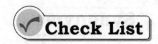
Check List

(   ) 1. astronaut   A. earlier

(   ) 2. asylum   B. freely

(   ) 3. attach   C. kind

(   ) 4. attention   D. access

(   ) 5. attract   E. prohibit

(   ) 6. attribute   F. invite

(   ) 7. authentic   G. cosmonaut

(   ) 8. autonomously   H. feature

(   ) 9. avenue   I. sanctuary

(   ) 10. ban   J. insolvency

(   ) 11. bankruptcy   K. ascribe

(   ) 12. barricade   L. disabled

(   ) 13. bedridden   M. notice

(   ) 14. beforehand   N. blockade

(   ) 15. benevolently   O. original

Vocabulary Ratings

5–7 *Good*   8–11 *Very Good*   12–15 *Excellent*

Synonyms

1. astronaut
= cosmonaut

2. asylum
= sanctuary

3. attach
= ascribe

4. attention
= notice

5. attract
= invite

6. attribute
= feature
= trait

7. authentic
= original

8. autonomously
= freely

9. avenue
= access

10. ban
= prohibit
= veto

11. bankruptcy
= insolvency
= liquidation

12. barricade
= blockade

13. bedridden
= disabled

14. beforehand
= earlier
= previously

15. benign
= kind
= harmless

bilateral 〔 baɪˈlætərəl 〕 *adj.* 雙方的

The two countries have arrived at a *bilateral* agreement.

（79 政大）

```
bi  + later + al
|      |      |
two + side + adj.
```

bizarre 〔 bɪˈzɑr 〕 *adj.* 怪異的

The *bizarre* weather extremes have brought drought in the rainy season. （90 輔大）

blare 〔 blɛr 〕 *v.* 發出響聲

I can't stand it when the loud music *blares* from my neighbor's windows. （79 師大）

bleak 〔 blik 〕 *adj.* 荒涼的

The Great Basin, the *bleakest* desert in the United States, is practically devoid of trees. （84 政大）

blizzard 〔ˈblɪzəd〕*n.* 暴風雪

Blizzards cause power failures in the Northeast every winter. (84 中正)

block 〔 blɑk 〕*v.* 妨礙；阻擋

Trees that *block* the view of oncoming traffic should be cut down. (84 中正)

blotting paper   *n.* 吸墨紙

Oh, brother! I've spilt the ink and haven't got any *blotting paper*. (90 花師)

blunder 〔ˈblʌndə〕*n.* 錯誤 (= *mistake*)

Diplomatic misunderstandings can often be traced back to *blunders* in translation. (85 中興)

boycott 〔ˈbɔɪˌkɑt〕*v.* 聯合抵制

A lot of people are *boycotting* that store.

(81 淡江)

break 〔 brek 〕 *n.* 中斷

There was a sudden *break* in transmission during the newscast. (90花師)

brood 〔 brud 〕 *v.* 沉思 (= *think silently*)

He sat at his desk, *brooding* over why she had left him. (85中興)

budget 〔'bʌdʒɪt 〕 *n.* 預算

The enormous *budget* deficit is a drain on the country's economy. (82中興)

C

capacity 〔 kə'pæsətɪ 〕 *n.* 容量

The truck was equipped with a fuel tank which had a *capacity* of 140 liters. (87台大)

capitalize 〔'kæpətḷ,aɪz 〕 *v.* 利用

She *capitalizes* on her connections to promote her cosmetics business. (90台大)

capriciously 〔 kə'prɪʃəslɪ 〕 *adv.* 善變地

You can have no security when every person around you acts *capriciously*. (84 台大)

capture 〔 'kæptʃɚ 〕 *v.* 捕捉

The primary goal of this study is to *capture* the use of human language in contexts. (88 台大)

cataclysm 〔 'kætə,klɪzəm 〕 *n.* (政治社會的) 劇變 (= *disaster*)

The impoverished family could not withstand another *cataclysm*. (79 政大)

cautiously 〔 'kɔʃəslɪ 〕 *adv.* 謹慎地

The research was intelligently designed, expertly executed, and *cautiously* interpreted.

(90 台北)

celebrity 〔 sə'lɛbrətɪ 〕 *n.* 名人

John has posters of many Hollywood *celebrities* on his wall. (89 逢甲)

censor 〔'sɛnsɚ〕 v. 審查刪除

The film has been *censored* because of its
obscene content. (89 東華)

central 〔'sɛntrəl〕 *adj.* 中心的

The *central* point of Peter's dissertation is
that the world population is increasing. (84 交大)

certify 〔'sɝtə,faɪ〕 v. 證明 (= *affirm*)

A psychiatrist *certified* that the applicant
suffered from a mental disorder. (85 中興)

chance 〔tʃæns〕 *n.* 可能性 (= *possibility*)

There is a *chance* that his proposal will be
accepted. (80 中正)

channel 〔'tʃænl̩〕 v. 鑿渠；導向

If you *channel* your anger constructively,
your life will become much easier. (84 台大)

chaos 〔'keɑs 〕 *n.* 混亂

The citywide blackout caused *chaos*.

（81 交大）

charge 〔 tʃɑrdʒ 〕 *v.* 索價；收費

A pen like this usually costs $10, but they only *charged* me $8 for it. （81 中山）

cherish 〔'tʃɛrɪʃ 〕 *v.* 珍惜

Although she never went back to Japan, she *cherished* the memory of her stay there.

（89 東華）

choke 〔 tʃok 〕 *v.* 使窒息

He grabbed her by the throat and almost *choked* the life out ot her. （83 中興）

chop 〔 tʃɑp 〕 *v.* 砍

To *chop* means to cut into small bits with a knife. （79 師大）

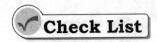

Check List

( ) 1. bilateral   A. error

( ) 2. bizarre   B. ponder

( ) 3. bleak   C. weird

( ) 4. blizzard   D. seize

( ) 5. blunder   E. shun

( ) 6. boycott   F. snowstorm

( ) 7. break   G. two-sided

( ) 8. brood   H. upheaval

( ) 9. capacity   I. interruption

( ) 10. capitalize   J. variably

( ) 11. capriciously   K. desolate

( ) 12. capture   L. confirm

( ) 13. cataclysm   M. remove

( ) 14. censor   N. utilize

( ) 15. certify   O. volume

Vocabulary Ratings

5–7 *Good*   8–11 *Very Good*   12–15 *Excellent*

Synonyms

1. bilateral
   = two-sided

2. bizarre
   = weird

3. bleak
   = desolate

4. blizzard
   = snowstorm

5. blunder
   = error

6. boycott
   = shun
   = proscribe

7. break
   = interruption

8. brood
   = ponder

9. capacity
   = volume

10. capitalize
    = exploit
    = utilize

11. capriciously
    = unsteadily
    = variably

12. capture
    = seize

13. cataclysm
    = upheaval

14. censor
    = remove
    = suppress

15. certify
    = confirm
    = verify

chronic (ˈkrɑnɪk) *adj.* 習慣性的;長期的;
慢性的

Chronic complainers bemoan their jobs,
marriages or life in general. (83 淡江)

The children never get enough to eat, so they
suffer from *chronic* malnutrition. (90 市北師)

circumscribe (ˌsɝkəmˈskaɪb) *v.* 限制活動

The rules of the private school *circumscribed*
the daily activities of the students. (88 東華)

claim (klem) *v.* 奪走 (人命)(= *take*)

The earthquake *claimed* hundreds of lives.

(80 政大)

clash (klæʃ) *v.* 衝突

I couldn't attend the meeting because the
date *clashed* with my holidays. (85 台大)

classified 〔'klæsə,faɪd 〕 adj. 分類的

The *classified* advertisements in the newspaper listed many apartments for rent. (80 交大)

coach 〔 kotʃ 〕 n. 教練

When the *coach* will decide which of the two boys will play ? (90 世新)

coercion 〔 ko'ɝʃən 〕 n. 強迫

The judge ruled that the suspect's confession was invalid because it was gotten through *coercion*.

(90 台大)

co = com	+ erce	+ ion
together	+ restrain	+ n.

coherent 〔 ko'hɪrənt 〕 adj. 有條理的

We found the professor's talk on constitutional reform quite *coherent*.

(86 中興)

co	+ here	+ ent
together	+ stick	+ adj.

collaborate 〔 kə'læbə͵ret 〕 v. 合作

I will *collaborate* with someone I hate if he

has compassion for less

fortunate people. (85 銘傳)

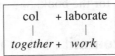

col	+ laborate
|	|
together +	*work*

collateral 〔 kə'lætərəl 〕 n. 抵押品

(= *guarantee*)

We did not get the loan because we didn't

have any *collateral*. (87 政大)

commercial 〔 kə'mɝʃəl 〕 adj. 商業的

This section of the city is zoned for

commercial buildings only. (80 中正)

commercialize 〔 kə'mɝʃəl͵aɪz 〕 v. 商業化

Movies out of Hollywood have typically

been very *commercialized*. (88 世新)

commission 〔 kə'mɪʃən 〕 v. 委託製作

I *commissioned* the artist to draw the picture for the book. (84 台大)

commit 〔 kə'mɪt 〕 v. 犯 (罪)

It is hoped that fear of punishment will prevent people from *committing* crimes. (89 逢甲)

commitment 〔 kə'mɪtmənt 〕 n. 誓約
(= *obligation*)

Every male citizen must make a two-year *commitment* to the army. (80 政大)

commodity 〔 kə'mɑdətɪ 〕 n. 貨物；商品

Investors buy large amounts of *commodities* and hope that the price increases. (85 逢甲)

compel 〔 kəm'pɛl 〕 v. 強迫

We planned to go on a picnic, but the rain *compelled* us to stay indoors. (82 中山)

competent〔'kɑmpətənt〕*adj.* 能勝任的

Mary was promoted because she is very *competent.*（87 台大）

competition〔,kɑmpə'tɪʃən〕*n.* 競爭

Collaboration is beginning to replace *competition* in many schools.（84 中正）

compile〔kəm'paɪl〕*v.* 編輯

Dan and Jenny are going to *compile* a list of all the places they want to visit.（87 逢甲）

com + pile
| |
together + heap

complementary〔,kɑmplə'mɛntərɪ〕*adj.* 互補的

We like to see men and women as *complementary* and not as antagonistic.

（90 台大）

compliment 〔'kɑmpləmənt 〕 v. 稱讚

The mayor *complimented* the fire fighters on their bravery. (90 義守)

comprise 〔 kəm'praɪz 〕 v. 由～組成；包含

A professor and three assistants *comprise* the task force. (91 世新)

The anthology *comprised* the best-known works of about twenty Victorian poets. (88 東華)

compromise 〔'kɑmprə,maɪz 〕 n. 安協

If you can't get your child to accept your suggestion, try to reach a *compromise* with him. (88 台大)

com	+ pro	+ mise
together	+ forth	+ throw

compulsory 〔 kəm'pʌlsərɪ 〕 adj. 強制的

English is a *compulsory* subject in undergraduate programs. (87 中正)

com	+ puls	+ ory
with	+ drive	+ adj.

Check List

(   ) 1. chronic   A. praise

(   ) 2. circumscribe   B. collide

(   ) 3. clash   C. consist of

(   ) 4. coercion   D. assign

(   ) 5. coherent   E. compulsion

(   ) 6. collateral   F. habitual

(   ) 7. commercialize   G. perpetrate

(   ) 8. commission   H. restrict

(   ) 9. commit   I. warranty

(   ) 10. compel   J. capable

(   ) 11. competent   K. rational

(   ) 12. compliment   L. obligatory

(   ) 13. comprise   M. force

(   ) 14. compromise   N. praise

(   ) 15. compulsory   O. deal

Vocabulary Ratings

5–7 *Good*   8–11 *Very Good*   12–15 *Excellent*

Synonyms

1. chronic
   = habitual

2. circumscribe
   = restrict

3. clash
   = collide

4. coercion
   = compulsion

5. coherent
   = rational

6. collateral
   = warranty
   = guarantee

7. commercial
   = trade

8. commission
   = assign

9. commit
   = perpetrate

10. compel
    = force
    = coerce

11. competent
    = capable
    = able

12. compliment
    = praise

13. comprise
    = consist of

14. compromise
    = settlement
    = deal

15. compulsory
    = obligatory
    = required

conceal 〔 kən'sil 〕 v. 隱藏 (= *disguise*)

Athletes learn to *conceal* their
disappointment when they lose. (84中正)

concerted 〔 kən'sɝtɪd 〕 adj. 一致的

The richer countries of the world should take
concerted action to help the poorer countries.

(90政大)

conclusively 〔 kən'klusɪvlɪ 〕 adv. 確定地

Medical research has *conclusively* identified
tobacco as a threat to smokers' health. (86交大)

concrete 〔 'kɑnkrit 〕 adj. 具體的

Give a *concrete* example of the abstract
statement, "Honesty is the best policy." (85逢甲)

condemn 〔 kən'dɛm 〕 v. 譴責

Was the government right to *condemn* the
latest wave of protests? (90政大)

condense ﹝ kən'dɛns ﹞ v. 濃縮

He was able to *condense* the long paragraph and express the same idea in half as many words. ﹝79 師大﹞

```
con  +  dense
  |        |
together + make thick
```

```
con  + done
  |      |
wholly + give
```

condone ﹝ kən'don ﹞ v. 寬恕

A teacher cannot *condone* laziness. ﹝84 政大﹞

conducive ﹝ kən'djusɪv ﹞ adj. 有助於

Mother found the waterbed *conducive* to a restful sleep. ﹝88 東華﹞

confederate ﹝ kən'fɛdərɪt ﹞ adj. 同盟的

The *Confederate* Army retreated during the winter in order to conserve its strength.
﹝90 世新﹞

```
con   + feder + ate
  |       |      |
together + league + adj.
```

confer 〔 kən'fɝ 〕 v. 商量;協議

If you don't understand the assignment, you
can *confer* with a classmate. (80 逢甲)

confidential 〔 kɑnfə'dɛnʃəl 〕 adj. 機密的

This information is marked *confidential*.

(84 交大)

confine 〔 kən'faɪn 〕 v. 限制

A good student usually does not *confine* his
learning to school work. (82 台大)

confine 〔 'kɑnfaɪn 〕 n. 界限

Once in a lifetime, perhaps, one escapes the
actual *confines* of the flesh. (83 淡江)

confirm 〔 kən'fɝm 〕 v. 確認 (= *verify*)

Travel agents will *confirm*
your reservation. (84 中正)

con	+ firm
|	|
wholly	+ *firm*

confiscate ('kɑnfɪsˌket) v. 沒收；充公

Without giving me advance notice, the police *confiscated* my property yesterday. (84 中興)

conform (kən'fɔrm) v. 符合；使一致

The actual plans did not *conform* to the original specifications.

(80 中山)

con	+ form
|	|
together + *form*	

confrontation (ˌkɑnfrən'teʃən) n. 對抗

We avoided a direct *confrontation* with the opposition by coming up with a compromise.

(87 政大)

con	+ front	+ aion
|	|	|
together + *face*	+ *n.*	

conglomerate (kən'glɑmərɪt) n. 聚合體

The population of the U.S. is a *conglomerate* of people from different ethnic backgrounds.

(86 中興)

congregate 〔'kɑŋgrɪˌget 〕 v. 聚集

Many species of fish have developed the
ability to *congregate*
in schools. (90政大)

con	+ gregate
together	+ collect

connection 〔 kə'nɛkʃən 〕 n. 關係

A close *connection* between smoking and
lung diseases has been found. (86台大)

connote 〔 kən'not 〕 v. 暗示；隱含

Nowadays, the word "individualism" seems
to *connote* selfishness. (90台大)

conscience 〔'kɑnʃəns 〕 n. 良心

Amy thought of doing a wicked thing, but her
conscience wouldn't
let her. (82中山)

con	+ sci	+ ence
with	+ know	+ n.

consensus 〔 kən'sɛnsəs 〕 *n.* 共識

The *consensus* among the scientists is that the world is going to continue to warm up.

（88 台大）

con	+ sens + us
|	| |
together	*+ feel + n.*

consider 〔 kən'sɪdɚ 〕 *v.* 考慮

Students should carefully *consider* the matter before entering graduate school. (84 中山)

considerable 〔 kən'sɪdərəbḷ 〕 *adj.* 相當大的

James Joyce had *considerable* influence on Irish literature in the twentieth century.

（82 台大）

consistent 〔 kən'sɪstənt 〕 *adj.* 符合的

This new advertising campaign is not *consistent* with our company policy. (85 台大)

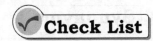
Check List

( ) 1. conceal   A. helpful

( ) 2. concerted   B. censure

( ) 3. conclusively   C. gather

( ) 4. concrete   D. consent

( ) 5. condemn   E. discuss

( ) 6. condense   F. hide

( ) 7. condone   G. allied

( ) 8. conducive   H. compact

( ) 9. confederate   I. huge

( ) 10. confer   J. intensive

( ) 11. conform   K. match

( ) 12. congregate   L. definitely

( ) 13. connote   M. imply

( ) 14. consensus   N. forgive

( ) 15. considerable   O. tangible

Vocabulary Ratings

5–7 *Good*   8–11 *Very Good*   12–15 *Excellent*

Synonyms

1. conceal
   = hide

2. concerted
   = intensive

3. conclusively
   = definitely

4. concrete
   = tangible

5. condemn
   = censure

6. condense
   = compact
   = compress

7. condone
   = forgive

8. conducive
   = helpful

9. confederate
   = allied

10. confer
    = consult
    = discuss

11. conform
    = match
    = correspond

12. congregate
    = gather

13. connote
    = imply

14. consensus
    = agreement
    = consent

15. considerable
    = huge
    = great

conspicuous 〔 kən'spɪkjʊəs 〕 *adj.* 顯著的

Traffic signs should be *conspicuous*, or
drivers will not be able to see them. (81 師大)

constitute 〔'kɑnstə,tjut 〕 *v.* 組成

Milk is a suspension of nourishing materials
in water, which *constitutes* about 86 percent
of the total weight.

(90 成大)

con	+ stitute
together	+ stand

consultation 〔,kɑnsḷ'teʃən 〕 *n.* 診斷

Most doctors today have a very
restricted area of *consultation*. (88 交大)

contagious 〔 kən'tedʒəs 〕 *adj.* 接觸傳染的

AIDS is a *contagious* disease, which means
that it is transmitted through bodily contact.

(85 銘傳)

con	+ tag	+ ious
together	+ touch	+ adj.

contention 〔 kən'tɛnʃən 〕 *n.* 爭論

It was the defense lawyer's *contention* that his client could not have committed the crime.

（ 83 台大 ）

contingency 〔 kən'tɪndʒənsɪ 〕 *n.* 可能性

Experiments based on this hypothesis are designed to test each *contingency*. （ 87 政大 ）

continuous 〔 kən'tɪnjʊəs 〕 *adj.* 連續的

All that is needed is a *continuous* supply of petroleum. （ 90 屏師 ）

contrast 〔'kɑntræst 〕 *n.* 對比

The *contrast* between the two different ways of living is important to bear in mind.

（ 81 逢甲 ）

contribute 〔 kən'trɪbjut 〕 *v.* 促成

Smoking has been found to *contribute* to the development of lung cancer. （ 88 台大 ）

control 〔 kən'trol 〕 *n.* 控制

· Cancer cells are cells that riot, growing and multiplying out of *control*. (88 台大)

controversial 〔,kɑntrə'vɝʃəl 〕 *adj.* 有爭議的

It's a *controversial* topic that arouses strong and often contradictory opinions. (80 交大)

```
contro  + vers + ial
  |         |      |
against  + turn + adj.
```

controversy 〔'kɑntrə,vɝsı 〕 *n.* 爭論

The design of wildlife refuges is still a matter of considerable *controversy*. (86 中興)

converge 〔 kən'vɝdʒ 〕 *v.* 集中於一點

The two roads *converge* just outside of town.

(83 淡江)

convert 〔 kən'vɜt 〕 v. 使轉變 (= *change*)

The function of ears in hearing is to *convert* sound waves to nerve impulses. (86 中興)

con	+ vert
|	|
together	+ *turn*

convertible 〔 kən'vɜtəbḷ 〕 adj. 敞篷的

That young man's favorite kind of car has a *convertible* top. (84 交大)

convict 〔 kən'vɪkt 〕 v. 判～有罪

After a suspect is *convicted* of murder, he or she may be given the death penalty.

(88 逢甲)

convince 〔 kən'vɪns 〕 v. 使確信

Joyce *convinced* her father that both she and her husband would be happy. (80 中山)

cordially 〔'kɔrdʒəlɪ 〕 *adv.* 熱忱地

The host and hostess *cordially* welcomed
their foreign guests. (83 交大)

correlate 〔'kɔrə,let 〕 *v.* 有相互關係

The amount of time students spend studying
correlates with their grades. (89 文化)

cor	+	re	+	late
together	+	back	+	bring

correspond 〔,kɔrɪ'spɑnd 〕 *v.* 通信

While I was away at school, I *corresponded*
regularly with my brothers and sisters. (87 台大)

counterfeit 〔'kaʊntəfɪt 〕 *adj.* 偽造的

A large amount of *counterfeit* money was
discovered at the scene. (81 清大)

counterpart 〔'kaʊntəˌpɑrt 〕 *n.* 相對應
的人或物

The U.S. president met his French
counterpart to discuss a
new agreement. (89 逢甲)

```
counter + part
   |        |
opposite + part
```

coup 〔 ku 〕 *n.* 政變

The *coup* attempt was unsuccessful in
overthrowing the government. (81 逢甲)

coverage 〔'kʌvərɪdʒ 〕 *n.* 報導

Local media organizations rely on foreign
news agencies for world news *coverage*.

(81 逢甲)

crave 〔 krev 〕 *v.* 渴望；想要

When a pregnant woman *craves* pickles,
it's probably because she needs salt to
retain water. (90 市北師)

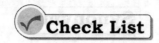
Check List

( ) 1. conspicuous   A. assure

( ) 2. constitute   B. amiably

( ) 3. contagious   C. sentence

( ) 4. contention   D. infectious

( ) 5. contingency   E. debatable

( ) 6. continuous   F. alter

( ) 7. controversial   G. compose

( ) 8. converge   H. obvious

( ) 9. convert   I. fake

( ) 10. convict   J. meet

( ) 11. convince   K. dispute

( ) 12. cordially   L. revolution

( ) 13. counterfeit   M. equal

( ) 14. counterpart   N. possibility

( ) 15. coup   O. constant

Vocabulary Ratings

5–7 *Good*   8–11 *Very Good*   12–15 *Excellent*

Synonyms

1. conspicuous
   = obvious

2. constitute
   = compose

3. contagious
   = infectious

4. contention
   = dispute

5. contingency
   = possibility

6. continuous
   = constant
   = nonstop

7. controversial
   = debatable

8. converge
   = meet

9. convert
   = alter

10. convict
    = sentence
    = condemn

11. convince
    = assure
    = persuade

12. cordially
    = amiably

13. counterfeit
    = fake

14. counterpart
    = equal
    = equivalent

15. coup
    = revolution
    = rebellion

credulous 〔 'krɛdʒələs 〕 *adj.* 輕信的

Maggie is *credulous*.

（86 政大）

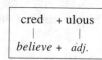

criteria 〔 kraɪ'tɪrɪə 〕 *n. pl.* 標準

What *criteria* did they employ when they
selected this picture as the prize-winner?

（90 花師）

crucial 〔 'kruʃəl 〕 *adj.* 非常重要的

It was a *crucial* decision. （81 淡江）

crystallize 〔 'krɪstḷ,aɪz 〕 *v.* 具體化

We need to *crystallize* our idea or thought
so that others will understand what we
intend to do. （88 銘傳）

cultivate 〔 'kʌltə,vet 〕 *v.* 培養

Parents should *cultivate* in their children a
desire to learn and the habit of reading. （87 台大）

curb 〔 kɝb 〕 *v.* 抑制 (= *restrain*)

The government should *curb* public spending.

(80 政大)

curtail 〔 kɝ'tel 〕 *v.* 縮減

Please *curtail* your spending this month.

(84 交大)

custody 〔 'kʌstədɪ 〕 *n.* 拘留

The defendant was kept in *custody* while awaiting trial. (90 成大)

D

dampen 〔 'dæmpən 〕 *v.* 使沮喪

Oddly enough, Tim's failure at badminton never *dampened* his enthusiasm. (84 政大)

daringly 〔 'dɛrɪŋlɪ 〕 *adv.* 勇敢地

Paul Revere *daringly* rode through the New England countryside to warn the colonists.

(90 世新)

decade 〔'dɛked 〕 n. 十年

Over the last *decade*, writer-director David
Mamet has made many
great films. (89 淡江)

deca + de
| |
ten + n.

deceitful 〔 dɪ'sitfəl 〕 adj. 虛偽的

Nothing is more *deceitful* than the
appearance of humility. (87 中正)

deceive 〔 dɪ'siv 〕 v. 欺騙

Misleading advertising may
deceive the public. (85 逢甲)

de   + ceive
| |
away + take

decennial 〔 dɪ'sɛnɪəl 〕 adj. 十年一度的

The national *decennial* census has been
nothing more than a simple headcount.

(81 淡江)

decide 〔 dɪ'saɪd 〕 *v.* 決定

Just as I got down to work, my friends
decided to visit me. (90 成大)

decidedly 〔 dɪ'saɪdɪdlɪ 〕 *adv.* 無疑地

The man looked *decidedly* uncomfortable.

(80 政大)

decision 〔 dɪ'sɪʒən 〕 *n.* 決定

They made their *decision* after making
careful calculations. (85 交大)

decline 〔 dɪ'klaɪn 〕 *v.* 拒絕

Carol *declined* Tim's offer to give her a ride
home. (90 屏師)

deem 〔 dim 〕 *v.* 認爲

The U.S. *deemed* peace talks between the
two countries necessary. (88 台大)

defective 〔 dɪ'fɛktɪv 〕 adj. 有瑕疵的

We will replace this *defective* lens with a perfect one. (85 逢甲)

deference 〔 'dɛfərəns 〕 n. 敬意；服從

Something about the statesman commands our instant response and *deference*. (84 中興)

de	+	fer	+	encee
down	+	carry	+	n.

defiance 〔 dɪ'faɪəns 〕 n. 反抗

The students gathered at the campus park in *defiance* of the curfew order. (81 交大)

de	+	fi	+	ance
apart	+	trust	+	n.

deficiency 〔 dɪ'fɪʃənsɪ 〕 n. 缺乏；不足

After years of *deficiency*, the unfortunate woman was forced to live in poverty. (90 師大)

defuse 〔 dɪˈfjuz 〕 *v.* 緩和 (= *reduce*)

The government should do something to *defuse* the crisis. (83 政大)

defy 〔 dɪˈfaɪ 〕 *v.* 違抗

Love *defies* age and religion. (83 中興)

de + fy	de + hydr + ation
| |	| | |
apart + trust	*away + water + n.*

dehydration 〔 ˌdihaɪˈdreʃən 〕 *n.* 脫水

After so many days in the desert, he was suffering from severe *dehydration*. (90 台大)

delay 〔 dɪˈle 〕 *v.* 延緩

We had better *delay* the work for a while.

(84 交大)

delete 〔 dɪˈlit 〕 *v.* 刪除

Would you please *delete* my name from the list? (90 屏師)

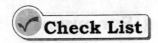

Check List

( ) 1. credulous   A. discourage

( ) 2. crucial   B. respect

( ) 3. cultivate   C. trusting

( ) 4. curb   D. soothe

( ) 5. custody   E. lying

( ) 6. dampen   F. vital

( ) 7. deceitful   G. consider

( ) 8. decide   H. resistance

( ) 9. decline   I. nurture

( ) 10. deem   J. flawed

( ) 11. defective   K. determine

( ) 12. deference   L. rebel

( ) 13. defiance   M. arrest

( ) 14. defuse   N. reject

( ) 15. defy   O. restrain

Vocabulary Ratings

5–7 *Good*   8–11 *Very Good*   12–15 *Excellent*

Synonyms

1. credulous
   = trusting

2. crucial
   = vital

3. cultivate
   = nurture

4. curb
   = restrain

5. custody
   = arrest

6. dampen
   = frustrate
   = discourage

7. deceitful
   = lying

8. decide
   = determine

9. decline
   = reject

10. deem
    = think
    = consider

11. defective
    = flawed
    = imperfect

12. deference
    = respect

13. defiance
    = resistance

14. defuse
    = soothe
    = cool

15. defy
    = rebel
    = disobey

deliberate〔 dɪˈlɪbəˌret 〕 v. 慎重考慮

The jury are *deliberating* the case.

（83 中興）

de	+ liberate
thoroughly +	*weigh*

deliberately〔 dɪˈlɪbərɪtlɪ 〕 adv. 故意地

Mary *deliberately* came home late to avoid
meeting her cousin. （84 交大）

delinquency〔 dɪˈlɪŋkwənsɪ 〕 n. 犯罪

Slums breed disease, juvenile *delinquency*,
and crime.

（89 成功）

de	+ linqu	+ ency
away +	*leave* +	*n.*

demeanor〔 dɪˈminɚ 〕 n. 行為舉止

His calm *demeanor* earned him the respect
and admiration of the other soldiers. （89 逢甲）

demolish〔dɪˈmɑlɪʃ〕v. 拆除

The government has declined to *demolish* the whole building. (90師大)

denigrate〔ˈdɛnəˌgret〕v. 貶低

His critical remark was an attempt to *denigrate* the value of our suggestion. (90台北)

depress〔dɪˈprɛs〕v. 使沮喪

When you *depress* someone, you make him or her sad. (90彰師大)

```
  de  + press          de  + ride
   |      |              |      |
 down + press         away + laugh
```

deride〔dɪˈraɪd〕v. 嘲笑

The politician *derided* the plan of his opponent, calling it nonsenses. (80中興)

derive 〔 də'raɪv 〕 v. 源自

It is amazing to think that so many languages *derive* from a common ancestor. (81 政大)

de + rive
| |
away + stream

de + sign + ate
| | |
down + mark + v.

designate 〔'dɛzɪg,net 〕 v. 命名

The southern territory was *designated* Louisiana after the French monarch King Louis XVI. (88 東華)

desultory 〔'dɛsḷ,torɪ 〕 adj. 散漫的

If you continue to work in that *desultory* way, you will never finish anything.

(79 政大)

de + sult + ory
| | |
off + leap + adj.

détente 〔 deˈtɑnt 〕 n.【法】國際上緊張關係之緩和

Nixon's negotiations with Soviet leaders led to a period of *détente*, or easing of tensions.

（82 中興）

detergent 〔 dɪˈtɝdʒənt 〕 n. 清潔劑

Detergent is a soap substitute used for washing and cleaning. （86 中興）

deteriorate 〔 dɪˈtɪrɪəˌret 〕 v. 惡化

It was obvious that his grandma's health was *deteriorating* after her surgery. （88 台大）

detest 〔 dɪˈtɛst 〕 v. 厭惡（ = *abhor* ）

Most students *detest* lengthy exams at the end of the year. （84 淡江）

detrimental 〔‚dɛtrə'mɛntḷ〕 *adj.* 有害的

Lack of exercise can have a *detrimental* effect
on your health.

（90 政大）

de	+ trim	+ ent	+ al
|	|	|	|
apart	+ *rub*	+ *n.*	+ *adj.*

developed 〔dɪ'vɛləpt〕 *adj.* 已開發的

Taiwan is now recognized as a *developed*
country.（86 逢甲）

devious 〔'divɪəs〕 *adj.* 不正直的

She used *devious* means to gain power.（83 台大）

de	+ vi	+ ous
|	|	|
away from	+ *way*	+ *adj.*

devise 〔dɪ'vaɪz〕 *v.* 想出；設計

The businessmen *devised* a good plan for
increasing sales.（84 交大）

dialogue 〔'daɪə‚lɔg 〕 *n.* 對話

The story contains an interesting *dialogue*
between the main characters.

（81清大）

dic	+	ion
say	+	*n.*

diction 〔'dɪkʃən 〕 *n.* 措辭；用語

Radio and television announcers study *diction*
so they can be clearly understood. （80逢甲）

dilapidate 〔 də'læpə‚det 〕 *v.* 荒廢；破損

The mayor plans to convert those *dilapidated*
buildings into a complex of fancy shops. （84中興）

di	+	lapid	+	ate
apart	+	*stone*	+	*v.*

di	+	lemma
double	+	*assumption*

dilemma 〔 də'lɛmə 〕 *n.* 左右爲難

Henry is in a dreadful *dilemma*. He loves his
wife, but he can't stand his wife's parents.

（86交大）

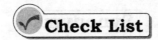

Check List

( ) 1. deliberate	A. entitle
( ) 2. delinquency	B. aimless
( ) 3. demeanor	C. reflect
( ) 4. demolish	D. worsen
( ) 5. designate	E. discourage
( ) 6. depress	F. mock
( ) 7. deride	G. crime
( ) 8. derive	H. despise
( ) 9. designate	I. behavior
( ) 10. desultory	J. originate
( ) 11. deteriorate	K. conceive
( ) 12. detest	L. dismantle
( ) 13. detrimental	M. wording
( ) 14. devise	N. defame
( ) 15. diction	O. harmful

Vocabulary Ratings

5–7 *Good*   8–11 *Very Good*   12–15 *Excellent*

Synonyms

1. deliberate
   = reflect

2. delinquency
   = crime

3. demeanor
   = behavior

4. demolish
   = dismantle

5. denigrate
   = defame

6. depress
   = discourage
   = sadden

7. deride
   = mock

8. derive
   = originate

9. designate
   = entitle

10. desultory
    = aimless
    = unfocused

11. deteriorate
    = worsen
    = decline

12. detest
    = despise

13. detrimental
    = harmful

14. devise
    = conceive
    = contrive

15. diction
    = phrasing
    = wording

diminish 〔 dəˈmɪnɪʃ 〕 v. 減少

With the perfection of modern communication systems, sign and signal language has *diminished* in importance. (88 逢甲)

$$
\begin{array}{ccc}
\text{di} & + \text{ mini } + & \text{sh} \\
| & | & | \\
\textit{intensive} & + \textit{ small } + & \textit{v.}
\end{array}
$$

dire 〔 daɪr 〕 *adj.* 極度的 (= *extreme*)

That boy is in *dire* need of psychiatric help.

(82 政大)

disabling 〔 dɪsˈeblɪŋ 〕 *adj.* 使殘廢的

Both hurricanes and tornadoes bring *disabling* winds. (85 交大)

disadvantage 〔 ˌdɪsədˈvæntɪdʒ 〕 v. 損害

He argues that women have been doubly *disadvantaged* by existing laws and customs.

(80 中興)

discernible 〔 dɪˈsɝnəbl̩ 〕 *adj.* 可辨別的

Something which can be seen or recognized
is *discernible*.

（87 淡江）

dis	+	cern	+ able
|		|	|
apart	+	*separate*	+ *adj.*

discharge 〔 dɪsˈtʃɑrdʒ 〕 *v.* 允許～離開

Hospitals usually do not *discharge* a patient
until the doctors think the patient is ready to
go home. （88 交大）

disclose 〔 dɪsˈkloz 〕 *v.* 透露

A gunman, whose name wasn't immediately
disclosed, injured a security guard. （85 清大）

disconcerting 〔 ˌdɪskənˈsɝtɪŋ 〕 *adj.* 擾亂的

Though stress symptoms may be *disconcerting*,
they are normal after a crisis or disaster.

（90 政大）

discourse〔 dɪˋskɔrs 〕 *n.* 交談

Civilized *discourse* between the two
countries has become impossible. (91 世新)

discrepancy〔 dɪˋskrɛpənsɪ 〕 *n.* 不一致
(= *difference*)

Cashiers must account for *discrepancies*
between money taken and the amount on
the register tape. (86 中興)

discriminate〔 dɪˋskrɪməˌnet 〕 *v.* 歧視

It is now unlawful to *discriminate* on the
basis of race, sex, or national origin.
(80 中山)

dis	+ drimin +	ate
apart	space	v.

discrimination〔 dɪˌskrɪməˋneʃən 〕 *n.*
歧視 (= *bias*)

Laws have been passed against sex
discrimination. (83 政大)

disdainfully 〔 dɪs'denfəlɪ 〕 *adv.* 傲慢地

Mrs. Lee looked at the other guests
disdainfully. (86 政大)

dismay 〔 dɪs'me 〕 *n.* 驚慌;沮喪

Jim's face was a picture of *dismay* when he
realized he'd left his bags in the bus station.

(81 中山)

dismiss 〔 dɪs'mɪs 〕 *v.* 不受理

Since there was not enough evidence the
judge *dismissed* the case. (90 世新)

disparaging 〔 dɪs'pærɪdʒɪŋ 〕 *adj.* 輕視
的;責難的 (= *deprecatory*)

Mary made some *disparaging* remarks
about Jane. (82 政大)

disposable 〔 dɪ'spozəbḷ 〕 *adj.* 用完即丟的

These paper plates are *disposable* after use.

(83 中興)

disposal 〔 dɪ'spozl̩ 〕 *n.* 處理

The scientist had at his *disposal* a fully equipped laboratory. (80 逢甲)

disproportionately 〔 ˌdɪs'porʃənɪtlɪ 〕 *adv.* 不成比例地 (= *unequally*)

The United States Congress has two houses so that the large states will not be *disproportionately* represented. (87 中興)

dispute 〔 dɪ'spjut 〕 *v.* 爭論；爭辯 (= *argue*)

Economists *disputed* whether consumer spending was as strong as the figure suggested. (86 中興)

disregard 〔 ˌdɪsrɪ'gɑrd 〕 *v.* 忽視；不注意

People who *disregard* a traffic law may have their driver's license suspended. (84 中山)

dis	+	re	+	gard
not	+	*again*	+	*watch*

distaste 〔 dɪs'test 〕 *n.* 嫌惡

The famous director expressed his *distaste* for certain kinds of cheaply produced movies. (85 台大)

distinguish 〔 dɪs'tɪŋgwɪʃ 〕 *v.* 分辨

Some people have so little conscience that they can't *distinguish* between right and wrong. (81 中山)

diversity 〔 daɪ'vɝsətɪ 〕 *n.* 多樣性

The *diversity* of customs and social structures argues against the existence of a single Native American culture. (90 屏師)

divert 〔 daɪ'vɝt 〕 *v.* 使轉向 (= *distract*)

The noise from the street *diverted* his mind from studying. (85 中興)

Check List

( ) 1. dire   A. reveal

( ) 2. discernible   B. difference

( ) 3. disclose   C. dislike

( ) 4. disconcerting   D. disturbing

( ) 5. discourse   E. argue

( ) 6. discrepancy   F. extreme

( ) 7. discrimination   G. variety

( ) 8. disdainfully   H. dialogue

( ) 9. dismay   I. noticeable

( ) 10. disparaging   J. distract

( ) 11. dispute   K. critical

( ) 12. disregard   L. bias

( ) 13. distaste   M. ignore

( ) 14. diversity   N. panic

( ) 15. divert   O. scornfully

Vocabulary Ratings

5–7 *Good*   8–11 *Very Good*   12–15 *Excellent*

Synonyms

1. dire
   = extreme

2. discernible
   = noticeable

3. disclose
   = reveal

4. disconcerting
   = disturbing

5. discourse
   = dialogue

6. discrepancy
   = incongruity
   = difference

7. discrimination
   = bias

8. disdainfully
   = scornfully

9. dismay
   = panic

10. disparaging
    = scornful
    = critical

11. dispute
    = argue
    = debate

12. disregard
    = ignore

13. distaste
    = dislike

14. diversity
    = variety
    = change

15. divert
    = distract
    = avert

docile (ˈdɑsɪl) *adj.* 溫順的

One way to keep the citizenry *docile* is to
limit the means by which the
intellectuals can agitate. (87 淡江)

doc	+	ile
teach	+	*adj.*

documentary (dɑkjəˈmɛntərɪ) *n.* 紀錄片

Mr. Young is a film-maker, and he makes
documentaries. (84 交大)

dodge (dɑdʒ) *v.* 逃避 (= *evade*)

It is illegal to *dodge* taxes. (83 政大)

domesticate (dəˈmɛstəˌket) *v.* 馴養

Animals were first *domesticated* as a source
of food. (88 東華)

domesticated (dəˈmɛstəˌketɪd) *adj.* 馴服的

Of all the wild dogs, none is more closely
related to the *domesticated* dog than the
wolf. (80 淡江)

dominant ('dɑmənənt) *adj.* 支配的

He is one of the best scientists in physics and

plays a *dominant* role in
the field. (87 台大)

domi + nant
rule + adj.

dominate ('dɑməˌnet) *v.* 在～中佔主要地位

Unemployment, terrorism, and war *dominate*
today's headlines. (88 交大)

donate ('donet) *v.* 捐贈

Wealthy people regularly *donate* large

portions of their wealth to
charity. (90 彰師大)

don + ate
give + v.

downsize ('daʊnˌsaɪz) *v.* 縮小

When IBM *downsized* in 1995, it laid off
employees. (85 銘傳)

drastic ﹝'dræstɪk﹞ adj. 激烈的

We are going to have to do something *drastic* about the situation. (81師大)

drawback ﹝'drɔ,bæk﹞ n. 缺點

Many pure metals are too soft, rust too easily, or have some other *drawbacks*. (87中興)

drought ﹝draʊt﹞ n. 乾旱

Los Angeles has floods in some years, in others *drought*. (90屏師)

dual ﹝'djuəl﹞ adj. 雙重的 (= *twofold*)

Maria's career involves a *dual* role for her as a counselor and a teacher.

(90中正)

```
du + al
 |    |
two + adj.
```

dubious ﹝'djubɪəs﹞ adj. 可疑的

The claim that there was life on Mars seemed to us *dubious*. (87台大)

dumbfounded 〔͵dʌmˈfaʊndɪd 〕 *adj.* 嚇得目瞪口呆的 (= *speechless*)

When the protester entered the meeting clad only in a beach towel, the audience was *dumbfounded*. (90 中正)

duplicate 〔ˈdjupləkɪt 〕 *n.* 複製品

Would you mind making a *duplicate* of this for me? (81 淡江)

du + plic + ate
| | |
two + fold + n.

E

echo 〔ˈɛko 〕 *v.* 使迴響；重覆

His speech *echoed* my own feelings. (80 政大)

edible 〔ˈɛdəbḷ 〕 *adj.* 可食的

We have to know the difference between *edible* and poisonous berries. (83 中興)

efface 〔 ɪ'fes 〕 *v.* 抹去 (= *erase*)

Nothing could *efface* their memory of his
cruelty although many years
had elapsed. (84 淡江)

```
ef  + face
 |     |
out + face
```

efficacy 〔 'ɛfəkəsɪ 〕 *n.* 功效

The reporter questioned the *efficacy* of such
cold remedies. (86 政大)

efficiency 〔 ə'fɪʃənsɪ 〕 *n.* 效率

The increase in the output of Factory B is
due to the *efficiency* of its production
methods. (85 逢甲)

efficient 〔 ɪ'fɪʃənt 〕 *adj.* 有效率的

His secretary is pretty, smart, and *efficient*;
her Achilles' heel is her quick temper. (89 淡江)

elaborate 〔 ɪ'læbəˌret 〕 v. 詳述

Just tell us the facts and don't *elaborate*

on them. (81 中山)

e	+ labor	+ ate
|	|	|
out	+ *work*	+ *v.*

elated 〔 ɪ'letɪd 〕 *adj.* 興高采烈的

The long-distance runner was *elated* when he
learned that he had set a new record. (79 師大)

eliminate 〔 ɪ'lɪməˌnet 〕 v. 消除

Together let us explore the stars, conquer the
deserts, and *eliminate* diseases. (87 政大)

e	+ limin	+ ate
|	|	|
out	+ *threshold*	+ *v.*

elite 〔 ɪ'lit 〕 *adj.* 精英的

Many parents prefer to send their children to
an *elite* school for better education. (88 逢甲)

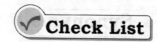

Check List

( ) 1. docile   A. twofold

( ) 2. dodge   B. trim

( ) 3. domesticate   C. expand

( ) 4. dominant   D. avoid

( ) 5. downsize   E. thrilled

( ) 6. drastic   F. tractable

( ) 7. dual   G. doubtful

( ) 8. dubious   H. radical

( ) 9. duplicate   I. remove

( ) 10. efface   J. tame

( ) 11. efficacy   K. copy

( ) 12. elaborate   L. best

( ) 13. elated   M. governing

( ) 14. eliminate   N. erase

( ) 15. elite   O. function

Vocabulary Ratings

5–7 *Good*   8–11 *Very Good*   12–15 *Excellent*

Synonyms

1. docile
   = tractable

2. dodge
   = avoid

3. domesticate
   = tame

4. dominant
   = governing

5. downsize
   = trim

6. drastic
   = radical
   = severe

7. dual
   = twofold

8. dubious
   = doubtful

9. duplicate
   = copy

10. efface
    = erase
    = delete

11. efficacy
    = use
    = function

12. elaborate
    = expand

13. elated
    = thrilled

14. eliminate
    = remove
    = cancel

15. elite
    = best
    = top

eloquent 〔'ɛləkwənt〕 adj. 雄辯的

Everyone was impressed by the *eloquent* speaker. (89東華)

e	+ loqu	+ ent
|	|	|
out	+ *speak*	+ *adj.*

embezzlement 〔ɪm'bɛzḷmənt〕 n. 挪用公款

The prisoner was accused of robbery, assault, *embezzlement* and forgery. (90世新)

emend 〔ɪ'mɛnd〕 v. 修訂 (= *correct*)

The passage in the book was *emended* before printing. (90交大)

emerge 〔ɪ'mɝdʒ〕 v. 出現

The chicks *emerged* slowly from the eggs.

(82淡江)

emerging 〔ɪ'mɝdʒɪŋ〕 adj. 出現的

The *emerging* democracies in the east bloc offer a chance for opposition parties come to power. (82台大)

emigrate 〔'ɛmə,gret 〕 v. 移民

Her parents *emigrated* from Taiwan to the
United States when she was six years old.

（81 師大）

e + migr + ate
| | |
out + remove + v.

e + miss + ion
| | |
out + send + n.

emission 〔 ɪ'mɪʃən 〕 n. 排出物

All cars must have devices to reduce exhaust
emissions. （80 政大）

emit 〔 ɪ'mɪt 〕 v. 發射（= *discharge*）

The purpose of the telescope is to gather light
that has been *emitted* by distant sources.

（89 台大）

emphasis 〔'ɛmfəsɪs 〕 n. 強調

Some people have been criticized for placing
too much *emphasis* on being on time. （84 中正）

employer 〔 ɪmˈplɔɪɚ 〕 *n.* 雇主 (= *boss*)

The worker has been dismissed by his *employer*. (80 中正)

encirclement 〔 ɪnˈsɝkl̩mənt 〕 *n.* 包圍

The use of roadblocks is simply an adaptation of the military concept of *encirclement*. (89 成功)

encumber 〔 ɪnˈkʌmbɚ 〕 *v.* 阻礙

Encumbered by our baggage, we almost missed the bus. (88 東華)

enforce 〔 ɪnˈfors 〕 *v.* 實施

The problem reflected the government's inability to *enforce* its laws and regulations.

(81 交大)

engrossed 〔 ɪnˈgrost 〕 *adj.* 全神貫注的

John was so *engrossed* in his novel that he forgot his appointment with his doctor. (84 淡江)

enhance 〔 ɪn'hæns 〕 v. 增進；提高

Helen's natural beauty was *enhanced* by her personality. (88 東華)

enormity 〔 ɪ'nɔrmətɪ 〕 n. 殘暴

The man did not grasp the *enormity* of betraying his comrades in arms. (83 台大)

```
en  + norm + ity
 |      |      |
out +  rule  +  n.
```

enroll 〔 ɪn'rol 〕 v. 入學

In 1978, Yale Law School *enrolled* 170 students from an applicant pool of 3700.

(84 台大)

ensure 〔 ɪn'ʃur 〕 v. 確保

The first duty of the state is to *ensure* that law-abiding people are protected form crime.

(81 交大)

enthusiasm 〔 ɪn'θjuzɪˌæzəm 〕 *n.* 熱忱

John loves to study, and he does all his schoolwork with *enthusiasm*. (82 中山)

enthusiastic 〔 ɪnˌθjuzɪ'æstɪk 〕 *adj.* 充滿熱忱的

He wrote an *enthusiastic* letter to the director of the research center. (81 逢甲)

entrenched 〔 ɪn'trɛntʃt 〕 *adj.* 根深蒂固的 (= *ingrained*)

Many people had been out of work for a long time because of the *entrenched* joblessness.

(88 政大)

environment 〔 ɪn'vaɪrənmənt 〕 *n.* 環境

The new park is a wonderful addition to the urban *environment*. (84 政大)

ephemeral 〔 ə'fɛmərəl 〕 *adj.* 短暫的

As an adolescent he had an intense but *ephemeral* passion for collecting postcards.

(88 東華)

ep	+ hemer	+ al
upon +	day	+ adj.

epidemic 〔ˌɛpə'dɛmɪk 〕 *n.* 傳染病

The recent *epidemic* of foot-and-mouth disease caused many people to avoid eating pork. (86 逢甲)

epitome 〔 ɪ'pɪtəmɪ 〕 *n.* 摘要

We only had time to read the *epitome* of your report. (84 交大)

epi	+ tome
upon +	cut

epoch 〔'ɛpək 〕 *n.* 時期

The music is typical of the *epoch* in which it was composed. (80 淡江)

Check List

(   ) 1. eloquent   A. hinder

(   ) 2. embezzlement   B. abstract

(   ) 3. emerge   C. impose

(   ) 4. emigrate   D. theft

(   ) 5. emit   E. absorbed

(   ) 6. encumber   F. guarantee

(   ) 7. enforce   G. eagerness

(   ) 8. engrossed   H. appear

(   ) 9. enormity   I. discharge

(   ) 10. enroll   J. persuasive

(   ) 11. ensure   K. rooted

(   ) 12. enthusiasm   L. cruelty

(   ) 13. entrenched   M. register

(   ) 14. ephemeral   N. migrate

(   ) 15. epitome   O. fleeting

Vocabulary Ratings

5–7 *Good*   8–11 *Very Good*   12–15 *Excellent*

Synonyms

1. eloquent
   = persuasive

2. embezzlement
   = theft

3. emerge
   = appear

4. emigrate
   = migrate

5. emit
   = discharge

6. encumber
   = handicap
   = hinder

7. enforce
   = impose

8. engrossed
   = absorbed

9. enormity
   = cruelty

10. enroll
    = register
    = sign up

11. ensure
    = guarantee
    = warrant

12. enthusiasm
    = eagerness

13. entrenched
    = rooted

14. ephemeral
    = fleeting
    = brief

15. epitome
    = abstract
    = summary

erode 〔 ɪ'rod 〕 *v.* 侵蝕；損壞 (= *devastate*)

Any deterioration of U.S. technological
advantage can *erode* the bedrock of U.S.
military security. (88 政大)

erosion 〔 ɪ'roʒən 〕 *n.* 侵蝕

The *erosion* of the beach is due to the
incessant pounding of the waves. (90 屏師)

eruption 〔 ɪ'rʌpʃən 〕 *n.* 爆發

On May 8, 1902, a volcanic *eruption* took
place and destroyed
Saint-Pierre. (82 中興)

e	+	rupt	+	ion
out	+	break	+	*n.*

escalate 〔 'ɛskə,let 〕 *v.* 升高

When supplies of a given product are limited,
the price of that product *escalates*. (86 中興)

espousal 〔 ɪsˈpauzḷ 〕 *n.* 信奉；支持

The vice president has expressed her recent *espousal* of feminism. (90 交大)

essential 〔 əˈsɛnʃəl 〕 *n.* 必需品

Are you one of those women who feel that lipstick is one of the *essentials* of life? (89 文化)

ethnic 〔ˈɛθnɪk 〕 *adj.* 民族的

In the U. S., Hispanics and Chinese are some of the *ethnic* minorities. (81 交大)

evasive 〔 ɪˈvesɪv 〕 *adj.* 逃避的；難以捉摸的

Her manner was always very *evasive*; she would never look straight at me. (87 逢甲)

eventually 〔 ɪˈvɛntʃuəlɪ 〕 *adv.* 最後

The work took a long time to complete but we *eventually* finished it. (90 師大)

evolution 〔,ɛvə'luʃən〕 *n.* 進化

Brain size increased dramatically during
human *evolution*. (82台大)

e	+ volut	+ ion
out	+ roll	+ *n.*

ex	+ asper	+ ation
fully	+ *rough*	+ *n.*

exasperation 〔 ɪg,zæspə'reʃən 〕 *n.* 憤怒

The manager felt no *exasperation* at his
secretary's inadequate handling of her job.

(90政大)

exceed 〔 ɪk'sid 〕 *v.* 超過

You will have problems if the amount of
money that you spend *exceeds* the amount
that you earn. (86中興)

ex	+ ceed
out	+ go

excel 〔 ɪk'sɛl 〕 *v.* 擅長;勝過別人

Because he was so small, Larry could not
excel in sports. (82淡江)

exception 〔 ɪk'sɛpʃən 〕 *n.* 例外

It is regretted that there can be no *exception* to this rule. (85 台大)

exclusive 〔 ɪk'sklusɪv 〕 *adj.* 唯一的；專用的

Geometrical ideas correspond to more or less exact objects in nature, and these last are undoubtedly the *exclusive* cause of the genesis of those ideas. (89 台大)

ex + clu + sive
| | |
out + shut + adj.

The liberary designated one room for the *exclusive* use of graduate students. (90 台北)

execution 〔 ˌɛksɪ'kjuʃən 〕 *n.* 執行

Public administration consists of the *execution* of public policy by public authorities. (87 中興)

exhausted 〔 ɪgˈzɔstɪd 〕 *adj.* 筋疲力盡的

If a person feels "enervated," he is *exhausted*.

（87 淡江）

```
ex  + haust + ed
 |      |      |
out  + draw  + adj.
```

exhaustively 〔 ɪgˈzɔstɪvlɪ 〕 *adv.* 徹底地；
廣泛地（ = *thoroughly* ）

The detectives *exhaustively* interviewed the
residents of the neighborhood. （86 中興）

expand 〔 ɪkˈspænd 〕 *v.* 擴大

When you blow air into a ballon, it will
expand. （85 交大）

expect 〔 ɪkˈspɛkt 〕 *v.* 期待

We did not *expect* the performance to be as
excellent as it was. （84 台大）

expense 〔 ɪk'spɛns 〕 *n.* 費用；代價

People want to live comfortably at the *expense* of turning the Earth into a wasteland. (87 台大)

expiration 〔 ˌɛkspə'reʃən 〕 *n.* 期滿

It has been announced that the *expiration* date of this law will be the last day of July. (80 中山)

ex +	pir	+ ation
out +	*breathe +*	*n.*

explain 〔 ɪk'splen 〕 *v.* 解釋

The criminal tried to *explain* away the false signature, but it was clear that he was guilty.

(80 逢甲)

explicit 〔 ɪk'splɪsɪt 〕 *adj.* 明確的

Our instructions were quite *explicit*. (86 政大)

exploit 〔 ɪk'splɔɪt 〕 *v.* 開採

Man has already *exploited* many of Earth's resources. (88 世新)

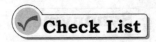

Check List

( ) 1. erode   A. precise

( ) 2. eruption   B. explosion

( ) 3. escalate   C. utilize

( ) 4. espousal   D. increase

( ) 5. essential   E. ambiguous

( ) 6. evasive   F. support

( ) 7. eventually   G. devastate

( ) 8. evolution   H. completion

( ) 9. exasperation   I. necessity

( ) 10. execution   J. wearied

( ) 11. exhausted   K. progression

( ) 12. expand   L. finally

( ) 13. expect   M. enlarge

( ) 14. explicit   N. anticipate

( ) 15. exploit   O. anger

Vocabulary Ratings

5–7 *Good*   8–11 *Very Good*   12–15 *Excellent*

Synonyms

1. erode
   = devastate

2. eruption
   = explosion

3. escalate
   = increase

4. espousal
   = support

5. essential
   = necessity

6. evasive
   = elusive
   = ambiguous

7. eventually
   = finally

8. evolution
   = progression

9. exasperation
   = anger

10. execution
    = completion
    = application

11. exhausted
    = wearied
    = worn out

12. expand
    = enlarge

13. expect
    = anticipate

14. explicit
    = precise
    = exact

15. exploit
    = utilize
    = develop

exploitation〔͵ɛksplɔɪ'teʃən〕*n.* 剝削

Compulsory education was instituted for the purpose of preventing the *exploitation* of children.（90 成大）

explore〔ɪk'splor〕*v.* 探險

The children loved *exploring* the old castles in England.（86 台大）

expose〔ɪk'spoz〕*v.* 使暴露

The Congressman resigned when the scandal was *exposed* to the public.（85 彰師）

```
ex + pose
 |     |
out + put
```

```
ex + quisite
 |     |
out + seek
```

exquisite〔'ɛkskwɪzɪt〕*adj.* 精緻的

He has *exquisite* taste in music.（83 淡江）

extensive ﹝ ɪk'stɛnsɪv ﹞ *adj.* 廣泛的

The government has called for *extensive* research on the social problems that have prevailed recently. (88 台大)

extradite ﹝'ɛkstrə,daɪt ﹞ *v.* 引渡

Attempts to *extradite* him from Taiwan were not pursued.

(85 中興)

ex + tradite
| |
out + surrender

F

facilitate ﹝ fə'sɪlə,tet ﹞ *v.* 使便利

An addressing machine *facilitates* the handling of bulk mail. (88 政大)

fallacy ﹝'fæləsɪ ﹞ *n.* 謬誤

Fallacies in argumentation are everywhere in the schools and in the mass media. (82 台大)

famine〔'fæmɪn〕 *n.* 饑荒

Famine is not a big problem in many European countries.（83交大）

fascinate〔'fæsn̩ˌet〕*v.* 使著迷

We were *fascinated* to see how skillfully the tennis player won the match.（82中山）

feasible〔'fizəbḷ〕*adj.* 可行的

People used to think it was impossible to live in outer space, but now it seems *feasible*.（88交大）

feature〔'fitʃɚ〕*n.* 特徵

Beautiful movie actresses with unusual *features* — such as dark, penetrating eyes, capture attention.（88交大）

fee〔fi〕*n.* 費用

Dr. Brown charges a high *fee* for his service.

（90彰師大）

felicitous 〔 fə'lɪsətəs 〕 *adj.* 幸福的；令人愉快的

On that *felicitous* occasion the amount of money he spent was irrelevant. (84 淡江)

fell 〔 fɛl 〕 *v.* 砍伐

The woodmen *felled* the trees two days ago.

(90 彰師大)

fertile 〔 'fɝtḷ 〕 *adj.* 肥沃的

The soil in which the plants are grown must be *fertile* in order to have a big crop. (81 中興)

figure 〔 'fɪgjɚ 〕 *v.* 認為

Scientists *figure* that the earth is billions of years old. (84 中山)

filament 〔 'fɪləmənt 〕 *n.* 纖維；細絲
(= *strand*)

A threadlike *filament* of a substance is called a fiber. (84 政大)

filial ﹝'fɪljəl﹞ *adj.* 子女的;孝順的

When a son does not treat his parents well, he
lacks *filial* consideration. (81 師大)

financier ﹝͵fɪnən'sɪr﹞ *n.* 財政家;金融業者

A person skilled in the management of
money, especially public money, is a
financier. (81 師大)

finite ﹝'faɪnaɪt﹞ *adj.* 有限的 (= *limited*)

Anything that can be counted is *finite*. (86 中興)

flabby ﹝'flæbɪ﹞ *adj.* (肌肉) 鬆弛的

Her *flabby* body was in great need of exercise.

(82 淡江)

flag ﹝ flæg ﹞ *v.* 衰退 (= *lag*)

At that time, Michael Jackson's image was
in tatters. His album sales were *flagging*.

(88 政大)

flaw 〔 flɔ 〕 *n.* 瑕疵

If a person gets in trouble due to his ideals instead of his own moral *flaws*, I will help him. (90 師大)

fledgling 〔ˋflɛdʒlɪŋ 〕 *n.* 生手

(= *greenhorn*)

As a pilot, he is still a *fledgling*. (83 政大)

flourish 〔ˋflɝɪʃ 〕 *v.* (事業等) 繁榮；興盛

The small French restaurant is *flourishing* and it's always crowded.

(88 交大)

```
flour  + ish
  |       |
flower + v.
```

fluently 〔ˋfluəntlɪ 〕 *adv.* 流利地

After living in France for two years, he could speak French *fluently*. (80 交大)

Check List

( ) 1. exploitation   A. practical

( ) 2. exquisite   B. wide

( ) 3. extensive   C. banker

( ) 4. extradite   D. loose

( ) 5. fallacy   E. transfer

( ) 6. famine   F. charge

( ) 7. feasible   G. novice

( ) 8. fee   H. abuse

( ) 9. felicitous   I. decline

( ) 10. fertile   J. starvation

( ) 11. figure   K. fine

( ) 12. financier   L. productive

( ) 13. flabby   M. error

( ) 14. flag   N. believe

( ) 15. fledgling   O. pleasant

Vocabulary Ratings

5–7 *Good*   8–11 *Very Good*   12–15 *Excellent*

Synonyms

1. exploitation
   = abuse

2. exquisite
   = fine

3. extensive
   = wide

4. extradite
   = transfer

5. fallacy
   = error

6. famine
   = starvation
   = scarcity

7. feasible
   = practical

8. fee
   = charge

9. felicitous
   = pleasant

10. fertile
    = productive
    = rich

11. figure
    = believe
    = think

12. financier
    = banker

13. flabby
    = loose

14. flag
    = lag
    = decline

15. fledgling
    = novice
    = beginner

foliage (ˈfolɪɪdʒ) *n.* 葉子 (= *leaves*)

Many tourists are attracted to Mt. Ali
by the autumn *foliage*.

（84 中興）

foli + age
| |
leaf + *n.*

forfeit (ˈfɔrfɪt) *v.* 喪失 (權力)

Several Taiwanese weightlifters *forfeited* their
right to compete in the 2000 Olympics due to
alleged drug abuse. （90 台大）

forgive (fəˈgɪv) *v.* 寬恕；原諒

We had a quarrel, I know. But let's just
forgive and forget. （81 中山）

formulate (ˈfɔrmjə͵let) *v.* 有系統地陳
述；明確地表達

The question of immortality is traditionally
formulated as a question about the soul or
the spirit of man. （81 中興）

fragile 〔ˈfrædʒəl〕 *adj.* 易碎的

With age, human bones
become more *fragile*.

（90 屏師）

```
frag + ile
  |     |
break + adj.
```

franchise 〔ˈfræntʃaɪz〕 *n.* 參政權

In England, women were given the *franchise*
in 1918. （83 中興）

fraudulent 〔ˈfrɔdʒələnt〕 *adj.* 騙人的

（ = *phony* ）

College registrars say they deal with
fraudulent claims at the rate of about
one per week. （87 政大）

free 〔 fri 〕 *adj.* 自在的

If we can be of further help, please feel *free*
to call on us at any time. （89 台大）

frightened 〔'fraɪtn̩d〕 *adj.* 害怕的

We were *frightened* by the noise in the forest.

（86台大）

frugal 〔'frugl̩〕 *adj.* 節省的

Mr. Connors is a very *frugal* man. （90義守）

frustrated 〔'frʌstretɪd〕 *adj.* 失敗的

Jack was *frustrated* in his attempt to become an actor. （87中正）

fundamentally 〔,fʌndə'mɛntl̩ɪ〕 *adv.*
基本上；本質上

The new manager reorganized the company, but nothing has *fundamentally* changed.

（90政大）

futile 〔'fjutl̩〕 *adj.* 徒勞的

The sailors made a *futile* attempt to save the ship. （87淡江）

G

gadget 〔'gædʒɪt 〕 *n.* 裝置；器具

Her kitchen has every *gadget* invented to make the housewife's work easier. (86 政大)

galaxy 〔'gæləksɪ 〕 *n.* 銀河

The *galaxy* to which our solar system belongs is also called the Milky Way. (83 中興)

gap 〔 gæp 〕 *n.* 間隔；間隙

This is just a temporary job to fill the *gap* between college and his studies abroad.

(90 彰師大)

gauzy 〔'gɔzɪ 〕 *adj.* 淡淡的

Rounding out the album are several instrumental pieces evoking an air of *gauzy* melancholy. (89 淡江)

gear 〔 gɪr 〕 *v.* 使適合 *< to >*

The textbook is *geared* to the readers' needs and level of proficiency. (90 台大)

generalize 〔'dʒɛnərəl,aɪz 〕 *v.* 推廣

In college, students learn to *generalize* from specific facts to larger situations. (89 台大)

general +	ize
總括的 +	*become*

genuine 〔'dʒɛnjuɪn 〕 *adj.* 眞正的

(= *authentic*)

Many countries restrict the exportation of *genuine* archeological artifacts. (86 中興)

geologist 〔 dʒɪ'ɑlədʒɪst 〕 *n.* 地質學家

Geologists are the scientists who study the earth itself. (82 中興)

geo +	log +	ist
earth +	*speak* +	人

germane 〔 dʒɝˈmen 〕 *adj.* 有關聯的

The facts were not *germane* to the argument.

（88 東華）

germinate 〔ˈdʒɝməˌnet 〕 *v.* 發芽（= *sprout*）

The seed *germinates* in the ground,
producing only a short root to anchor the
stem. （80 淡江）

gerontocrat 〔ˌdʒɛranˈtakret 〕 *n.* 年老的
官員

Western diplomats in Beijing argue that
China's *gerontocrats* will soon be replaced.

（84 中興）

given 〔ˈgɪvən 〕 *prep.* 就～而言
（ = *considering* ）

This department is the best place to study,
given my interest in finance and marketing.

（90 交大）

Check List

( ) 1. foliage
( ) 2. forfeit
( ) 3. formulate
( ) 4. fragile
( ) 5. fraudulent

( ) 6. frightened
( ) 7. frugal
( ) 8. futile
( ) 9. gadget
( ) 10. gauzy

( ) 11. gear (to)
( ) 12. genuine
( ) 13. germane
( ) 14. germanate
( ) 15. given

A. adapt (to)
B. terrified
C. granted
D. express
E. device

F. real
G. lose
H. leaves
I. light
J. thrifty

K. frail
L. phony
M. sprout
N. useless
O. relevant

Vocabulary Ratings

5–7 *Good*   8–11 *Very Good*   12–15 *Excellent*

Synonyms

1. foliage
   = leaves

2. forfeit
   = lose

3. formulate
   = express

4. fragile
   = frail

5. fraudulent
   = phony

6. frightened
   = terrified

7. frugal
   = thrifty

8. futile
   = useless

9. gadget
   = device

10. gauzy
    = light
    = thin

11. gear (to)
    = adapt (to)
    = adjust (to)

12. genuine
    = real

13. germane
    = relevant

14. germinate
    = sprout
    = bud

15. given
    = with
    = granted

gloomy 〔'glumɪ〕*adj.* 消沉的；沮喪的

Having failed in the final exam, he looked *gloomy* when he showed up this morning.

(80 中山)

gluttony 〔'glʌtṇɪ〕*n.* 貪吃；暴食
(= *overeating*)

Gluttony was once regarded as one of the seven deadly sins. (79 政大)

graft 〔 græft 〕*n.* (皮膚的) 移植

The plastic surgeon did a marvelous skin *graft* and now you can hardly see trace of the scar. (90 花師)

graphite 〔'græfaɪt〕*n.* 石墨

Lead pencils actually are made of *graphite* and not of lead. (91 清大)

grasp 〔 græsp 〕 *v.* 了解 (= *understand*)

The actor's duty is to *grasp* the full significance of life and to express it. (87 中正)

greed 〔 grid 〕 *n.* 貪婪 (= *avarice*)

King Midas's *greed* led him to spend a life of grief. (90 中正)

greedy 〔'gridɪ 〕 *adj.* 渴望的 (= *fervent*)

These students are *greedy* for knowledge.

(83 政大)

H

hacker 〔'hækɚ 〕 *n.* 駭客

It is important to prevent the intrusion of *hackers* into the computer network. (85 逢甲)

hamper 〔'hæmpɚ 〕 *v.* 妨礙 (= *impede*)

It took Paul a long time to write his report because he was *hampered* by his inability to type. (85 中興)

haphazard ('hæp'hæzəd) *adj.* 偶然的

Sometimes a *haphazard* event will stimulate
scientific research.

（86 逢甲）

hap +	hazard
|	|
luck +	*game of dice*

harass (hə'ræs) *v.* 使困擾；騷擾

In too many cases the government has
ignored, exploited, and *harassed* the
minority. (80 中山)

harassment (hə'ræsmənt) *n.* 騷擾

Men and women both need to raise their
awareness of sexual *harassment*. (88 銘傳)

harbinger ('hɑrbɪndʒə) *n.* 先驅；前兆

They see these as *harbingers* of a time when
machines will do all of the labor and man
will reap the benefits. (82 淡江)

harbour (ˈhɑrbɚ) *v.* 心懷

He *harbours* a secret wish to be a painter.

(83 中興)

harshness (ˈhɑrʃnɪs) *n.* 冷酷無情

All the working people spend 29 days of a month waiting for their pay day to arrive. It seems that all the *harshness* will be gone after they see the reward. (88 銘傳)

hazard (ˈhæzɚd) *n.* 危險

The company was willing to confront the sensitive issue of potential health *hazards* caused by their products. (90 政大)

hazardous (ˈhæzɚdəs) *adj.* 危險的

(= *perilous*)

The steep stairs look *hazardous*. (79 政大)

hectic ﹝ˈhɛktɪk﹞ *adj.* 緊張忙碌的

Rocking chairs and hammocks offer time out from a *hectic* life by slowing a rapid pace.

（90 政大）

hemisphere ﹝ˈhɛməsˌfɪr﹞ *n.* 半球

The left *hemisphere* of our brain is responsible for language, vision, the senses, and movement on the right side of the body.

（81 交大）

hemi + sphere	hence + forth
half + 球體	from here + towards

henceforth ﹝ˌhɛnsˈforθ﹞ *adv.* 今後

The library announced that *henceforth* fines on overdue books will be NT\$10 per day.

（86 中興）

hesitate ﹝ˈhɛzəˌtet﹞ *v.* 猶豫

If you *hesitate* too long, you may miss a wonderful opportunity. （85 台大）

heterogeneity 〔͵hɛtərədʒə'niətɪ〕 *n.* 異質

All that characterizes the United States--racial and ethnic *heterogeneity*, newness, vast territory, and individualistic ethics--is absent in Japan. (86 中興)

```
hetero   + gene + ity
  |          |      |
different + kind  + n.
```

hilarious 〔haɪ'lɛrɪəs〕 *adj.* 有趣的

That story Professor Lee told us two days ago was *hilarious*. (83 交大)

hinder 〔'hɪndə〕 *v.* 妨礙

The noise outside the office is *hindering* my work. (82 中山)

hinge 〔hɪndʒ〕 *v.* 取決於 < *on* >

A tobacco grower's income for the year may *hinge* on the good weather. (82 台大)

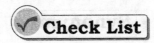

Check List

(   ) 1. gloomy   A. busy

(   ) 2. gluttony   B. hamper

(   ) 3. graft   C. avarice

(   ) 4. grasp   D. overeating

(   ) 5. greed   E. fervent

(   ) 6. greedy   F. funny

(   ) 7. hamper   G. impede

(   ) 8. haphazard   H. depressed

(   ) 9. harass   I. rest (on)

(   ) 10. harbinger   J. random

(   ) 11. harzardous   K. transplant

(   ) 12. hectic   L. annoy

(   ) 13. hilarious   M. understand

(   ) 14. hinder   N. omen

(   ) 15. hinge (on)   O. dangerous

Vocabulary Ratings

5-7 *Good*   8-11 *Very Good*   12-15 *Excellent*

Synonyms

1. gloomy
   = depressed

2. gluttony
   = overeating

3. graft
   = transplant

4. grasp
   = understand

5. greed
   = avarice

6. greedy
   = fervent
   = hungry

7. hamper
   = impede

8. haphazard
   = random

9. harass
   = torment

10. harbinger
    = forerunner
    = omen

11. hazardous
    = dangerous
    = perilous

12. hectic
    = busy

13. hilarious
    = funny

14. hinder
    = hamper
    = impede

15. hinge (on)
    = rest (on)

hoarse ﹝ hors ﹞ *adj.* 沙啞的 (= *husky*)

My classmate was *hoarse* from singing many folk songs all day long. (84 中興)

holocaust ﹝ˈhɑləˌkɔst﹞ *n.* 大破壞;大屠殺
(= *destruction*)

Hitler's *holocaust* of the Jews will never be forgotten. (83 交大)

homicide ﹝ˈhɑməˌsaɪd﹞ *n.* 殺人

The city police chief promised to look into the *homicide* case himself.

(91 彰師大)

homi + cide
| |
man + cut

homogeneous ﹝ˌhoməˈdʒɪnɪəs﹞ *adj.*
同性質的 (= *uniform*)

The fourth year sociology class was a *homogeneous* group of university students.

(90 中正)

horn 〔 hɔrn 〕 *n.* 喇叭

The driver blows the *horn* to make a loud warning noise. (79 師大)

hostile 〔'hɑstɪl 〕 *adj.* 有敵意的

The people in this village are *hostile* to outsiders because they don't trust any strangers.

(91 彰師大)

```
host    + ile
 |         |
hostility + adj.
```

hub 〔 hʌb 〕 *n.* 中心；中樞（ = *center* ）

Taiwan is presently establishing an Asia-Pacific Regional Operations Center with a view to becoming Asia's world business *hub*. (84 中興)

humane 〔 hju'men 〕 *adj.* 仁慈的；人道的

Dorothea Dix crusaded for the *humane* treatment of the mentally ill. (90 世新)

hybrid ﹝'haɪbrɪd﹞ *adj.* 雜種的

European observers sometimes classify him as a *hybrid* curiosity, neither fully American nor satisfactorily European. (81中興)

I

idolize ﹝'aɪdə,laɪz﹞ *v.* 把～視爲偶像

(= *worship*)

Most composers had not been *idolized* before they passed away. (84中興)

illiterate ﹝ɪ'lɪtərɪt﹞ *adj.* 文盲的

In mainland China, *illiterate* people comprise up to eighty percent of the population. (81交大)

il + literate
| |
not + 能讀寫的

illusion ﹝ɪ'luʒən﹞ *n.* 幻影；幻想

An optical *illusion* is a visual trick. (83中興)

illustrate ('ɪləstret) *v.* 說明

Professor Lee will give us an example to
illustrate this difficult
point in the next class.

（91 彰師大）

il	+	lustrate
on	+	*illuminate*

illustration (ˌɪləs'treʃən) *n.* 插圖；圖解 說明 (= *picture*)

Books with *illustrations* often give the
readers better ideas than those without them.

（87 中正）

immensely (ɪ'mɛnslɪ) *adv.* 極大地；非常

Your work has improved *immensely*. （81 淡江）

im	+	mense	+	ly
not	+	*measure*	+	*adv.*

im	+	merse
into	+	*sink*

immerse (ɪ'mɝs) *v.* 使熱中於

His followers, too, were deeply *immersed* in
the current disputations. （80 中興）

imminent 〔'ɪmənənt 〕 *adj.* 即將發生的

No one can be sure if the war is *imminent* or not. (84 中興)

im	+ min	+ ent
over ; opon	+ project	+ adj.

immunize 〔'ɪmjə‚naɪz 〕 *v.* 使免疫

The hospital *immunized* him against the disease. (84 交大)

impact 〔'ɪmpækt 〕 *n.* 影響

Some psychologists believe that television has a negative *impact* on children. (84 中山)

impartial 〔 ɪm'parʃəl 〕 *adj.* 公正的；無偏見的

I am sure her decision will be fair and just, for she has a reputation for being *impartial*.

(87 淡江)

impartiality 〔͵ɪmpɑrʃɪˈælətɪ〕 *n.* 公正

The girl did not want to take sides in the
argument between her two friends, but her
impartiality only made them both angry at her.

（89 台大）

impediment 〔 ɪmˈpɛdəmənt 〕 *n.* 缺陷

Mark cannot talk well because he has a
speech *impediment*. （90 中正）

im + pedi + ment	im + pend + ing
in + foot + n.	in + hang + adj.

impending 〔 ɪmˈpɛndɪŋ 〕 *adj.* 即將發生的

The dark clouds suggest an *impending*
storm. （83 政大）

imperative 〔 ɪmˈpɛrətɪv 〕 *adj.* 絕對必要的

It is *imperative* to stabilize Taiwan's political
and economic situation as soon as possible.

（89 淡江）

Check List

( ) 1. hoarse   A. center

( ) 2. holocaust   B. at hand

( ) 3. homogeneous   C. destruction

( ) 4. hostile   D. fair

( ) 5. hub   E. uniform

( ) 6. hybrid   F. mix

( ) 7. illiterate   G. delusion

( ) 8. illusion   H. husky

( ) 9. immensely   I. engross

( )10. immerse   J. vastly

( )11. imminent   K. adverse

( )12. impartial   L. coming up

( )13. impediment   M. drawback

( )14. impending   N. vital

( )15. imperative   O. uneducated

Vocabulary Ratings

5–7 *Good*   8–11 *Very Good*   12–15 *Excellent*

Synonyms

1. hoarse
   = husky

2. holocaust
   = destruction

3. homogeneous
   = uniform

4. hostile
   = adverse

5. hub
   = center

6. hybrid
   = mix
   = crossbreed

7. illiterate
   = uneducated

8. illusion
   = delusion

9. immensely
   = vastly

10. immerse
    = engross
    = engage

11. imminent
    = at hand
    = upcoming

12. impartial
    = fair

13. impediment
    = drawback

14. impending
    = coming up
    = coming

15. imperative
    = vital
    = crucial

imperfection 〔,ɪmpə'fɛkʃən 〕 *n.* 缺點
(= *defect*)

Sometimes items are put on sale because they
have *imperfections* in them. (84 中正)

implement 〔'ɪmpləmənt 〕 *v.* 實施

To prevent the epidemic from spreading,
certain policies must be *implemented*. (81 交大)

im + ple + ment
| | |
in + till + *n.*

im + pose
| |
on + put

impose 〔 ɪm'poz 〕 *v.* 把～強加於；強制執行

He did not enjoy playing cards every night,
but his friends *imposed* their tastes upon
him. (86 交大)

Hoping to become the first to break the trash
habit, Germany has *imposed* tough new
packaging rules. (81 逢甲)

impromptu 〔 ɪmˋprɑmptu 〕 *adj.* 即席的

Since Peter had not prepared any remarks, his talk was *impromptu*. (87 淡江)

impulse 〔ˋɪmpʌls 〕 *n.* 衝動

Those who act on *impulse* tend to make mistakes and feel regretful afterwards. (83 清大)

im + pulse
in + *push*

inaccessibility 〔ˏɪnækˏsɛsəˋbɪlətɪ 〕 *n.* 很難到達

The *inaccessibility* of the county offices forces the visitors to travel considerable distances. (87 淡江)

in + ac + cess + ibility
not + *to* + *go* + *n.*

incessantly 〔 ɪnˋsɛsəntlɪ 〕 *adv.* 不停地

Some work addicts don't want to work *incessantly*, but they just aren't able to stop.

(84 台大)

incident 〔'ɪnsədənt 〕 n. 事件

There were 17 reported *incidents* of high radiation exposure at nuclear plants between 1957 and 1988. (82台大)

inclination 〔ˌɪnklə'neʃən 〕 n. 傾向

Elderly people seem to have neither the chance nor the *inclination* to get plugged in. (90輔大)

in + clin + ation
in + bend + n.

incompatible 〔ˌɪnkəm'pætəbḷ 〕 adj. 不相容的；矛盾的

His religious belief is not *incompatible* with reason. (81中興)

in + com + pat + ible
not + together + suffer + adj.

incompetent 〔 ɪn'kɑmpətənt 〕 *adj.* 無能的
(= *incapable*)

Many weak and *incompetent* rulers were
overthrown. (90 中正)

incorporate 〔 ɪn'kɔrpə,ret 〕 *v.* 合併

Wells and Company are about to *incorporate*
with National Steel. (90 交大)

incorrigible 〔 ɪn'kɔrɪdʒəbḷ 〕 *adj.* 任性的

The Lee children were *incorrigible* last
Sunday evening. (86 政大)

incurable 〔 ɪn'kjʊrəbḷ 〕 *adj.* 無法治癒的

Many diseases formerly considered
incurable are now treated successfully. (90 成大)

indebted 〔 ɪn'dɛtɪd 〕 *adj.* 感激的

I am *indebted* to him for his valuable
comments on my article. (87 台大)

indicate 〔'ɪndə,ket〕 *v.* 意指

The flashing light *indicates* that there is some road construction ahead. (90世新)

in	+	dic	+ ate
towards	+	proclaim	+ *v.*

indicative 〔ɪn'dɪkətɪv〕 *adj.* 表示～的

There is an old saying that cold hands are *indicative* of a warm heart. (80逢甲)

indifferent 〔ɪn'dɪfərənt〕 *adj.* 漠不關心的

He was *indifferent* to success. He did not care about fame or monetary reward. (88台大)

in +	dif +	fer	+ ent
not +	apart +	carry	+ *adj.*

indigenous 〔ɪn'dɪdʒɪnəs〕 *adj.* 國產的

The exhibition presents the *indigenous* glass artworks of China. (89淡江)

indispensable 〔ˌɪndɪsˈpɛnsəbḷ〕 *adj.* 不可或缺的（ = *necessary* ）

It is *indispensable* to have a doctrine if only to avoid being deceived by false doctrines.

（87中正）

indoors 〔ˈɪnˈdorz〕 *adv.* 在室內

Tell your brother to come *indoors*, because it is going to rain very soon. （86台大）

industrious 〔 ɪnˈdʌstrɪəs 〕 *adj.* 勤勉的

In his biography, Thomas Hardy is described as a very *industrious* writer. （84中正）

industri + ous
| |
industry + adj.

inevitable 〔 ɪnˈɛvətəbḷ 〕 *adj.* 不可避免的

An argument is *inevitable* because they dislike each other so much. （91清大）

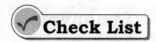
Check List

( ) 1. implement   A. signify

( ) 2. impose   B. enforce

( ) 3. impromptu   C. symbolic

( ) 4. impulse   D. spontaneous

( ) 5. incessantly   E. tendency

( ) 6. incident   F. execute

( ) 7. inclination   G. diligent

( ) 8. incurable   H. drive

( ) 9. indebted   I. native

( ) 10. indicate   J. fatal

( ) 11. indicative   K. ceaselessly

( ) 12. indifferent   L. obliged

( ) 13. indigenous   M. certain

( ) 14. industrious   N. apathetic

( ) 15. inevitable   O. event

Vocabulary Ratings

5–7 *Good*   8–11 *Very Good*   12–15 *Excellent*

Synonyms

1. implement
   = execute

2. impose
   = enforce

3. impromptu
   = spontaneous

4. impulse
   = drive

5. incessantly
   = ceaselessly

6. incident
   = event
   = occasion

7. inclination
   = tendency

8. incurable
   = fatal

9. indebted
   = obliged

10. indicate
    = imply
    = signify

11. indicative
    = symbolic
    = suggestive

12. indifferent
    = apathetic

13. indigenous
    = native

14. industrious
    = diligent
    = busy

15. inevitable
    = predictable
    = certain

inexplicable 〔 ɪnˈɛksplɪkəbḷ 〕 *adj.* 不能解釋的

The behavior of dogs is *inexplicable* to me because I cannot imagine what they think.

(90 台大)

infectious 〔 ɪnˈfɛkʃəs 〕 *adj.* 有傳染性的

Infectious diseases may be spread by viruses and bacteria. (86 中興)

infinitesimal 〔 ˌɪnfɪnəˈtɛsəmḷ 〕 *adj.* 微少的

Cobalt in *infinitesimal* amounts is one of the metals essential to life. (80 淡江)

inflame 〔 ɪnˈflem 〕 *v.* 激起

China's one-child-per-couple policy has *inflamed* the ancient preference for sons.

(82 台大)

inform 〔 ɪnˈfɔrm 〕 *v.* 通知

We should *inform* the committee of the change of plans. (89 台大)

infuriate 〔 ɪnˈfjʊrɪˌet 〕 v. 激怒 (= enrage)

The man's barking dog *infuriated* his neighbors because they could
not sleep. (88 政大)

in + furi + ate
in + *fury* + *v.*

ingenious 〔 ɪnˈdʒinjəs 〕 adj. 巧妙的
(= clever)

The magician's *ingenious* escape bewildered
the young audience. (79 政大)

ingredient 〔 ɪnˈgridɪənt 〕 n. 構成要素；
成分

The *ingredients* of a long and healthy life
include a good diet and exercise. (86 交大)

inhabit 〔 ɪnˈhæbɪt 〕 v. 居住

Antarctica is one of the most
sparsely *inhabited* areas on
earth. (84 中山)

in + habit
in + *have*

inherent 〔 ɪnˈhɪrənt 〕 *adj.* 固有的；與生俱來的

One of the problems *inherent* in having children is deciding how to educate them.

（81 政大）

inhibit 〔 ɪnˈhɪbɪt 〕 *v.* 制止

Please sing; do not let my listening *inhibit* you. （86 交大）

inimical 〔 ɪnˈɪmɪkl̩ 〕 *adj.* 有害的

Some people think that too much reliance on mechanical devices is *inimical* to health.

（87 淡江）

initial 〔 ɪˈnɪʃəl 〕 *adj.* 起初的；一開始的

The *initial* response to the proposal surprised the government officials. （86 中興）

initiate〔ɪˋnɪʃɪˏet〕*v.* 開始；創始（ = *begin* ）

The government will *initiate* the building's construction soon. (87 中正)

innovative 〔ˋɪnoˏvetɪv〕*adj.* 革新的

The *innovative* curriculum in New Zealand led to great success in teaching children reading and writing.

(82 台大)

in +	novate
in +	make new

innuendo 〔ˏɪnjʊˋɛndo〕*n.* 諷刺；影射

I am getting bored with her constant *innuendoes*. (86 政大)

inquisitive 〔ɪnˋkwɪzətɪv〕*adj.* 好問的

This student is very *inquisitive*.

(81 清大)

in +	quisit +	ive
into +	seek +	adj.

insinuate 〔 ɪnˈsɪnjuˌet 〕 v. 巧妙地指示

The news report *insinuated* that the mayor was bribed. (80 政大)

in + sinu + ate
| | |
into + curve + v.

in + spire
| |
into + breathe

inspire 〔 ɪnˈspaɪr 〕 v. 激勵

The desire for profit *inspires* manufacturers to change the design of their products each year. (84 中山)

instantaneous 〔ˌɪnstənˈtenɪəs 〕 adj. 瞬間的

The change was *instantaneous* after the doctor gave my brother the injection. (84 交大)

insurmountable 〔ˌɪnsɝˈmaʊntəbl̩ 〕 adj. 無法克服的

The country faces almost *insurmountable* difficulties in uniting its people. (90 政大)

intact〔ɪn'tækt〕*adj.* 完整無缺的

Archaeologists have uncovered the earliest
intact wall painting of the
Mayan civilization.

（90 台大）

```
in + tact
 |     |
not + touch
```

integrate〔'ɪntəˌgret〕*v.* 整合

When the new high school is completed,
the students of two smaller schools will
be *integrated*. (86 中興)

intelligence〔ɪn'tɛlədʒəns〕*n.* 聰明才智

The software engineer's *intelligence* was
limited to one area. (85 交大)

intention〔ɪn'tɛnʃən〕*n.* 意圖；打算

The government clearly had not the slightest
intention of changing the legislation. (85 台大)

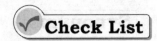

Check List

( ) 1. infectious	A. novel
( ) 2. infinitesimal	B. tiny
( ) 3. inflame	C. allude
( ) 4. infuriate	D. innate
( ) 5. inhabit	E. contagious
( ) 6. inherent	F. overtone
( ) 7. inhibit	G. motivate
( ) 8. inimical	H. prevent
( ) 9. initiate	I. arouse
( ) 10. innovative	J. inquiring
( ) 11. innuendo	K. enrage
( ) 12. inquisitive	L. detrimental
( ) 13. insinuate	M. populate
( ) 14. inspire	N. assimilate
( ) 15. integrate	O. start

Vocabulary Ratings

5–7 *Good*   8–11 *Very Good*   12–15 *Excellent*

Synonyms

1. infectious
   = contagious

2. infintesimal
   = tiny

3. inflame
   = arouse

4. infuriate
   = enrage

5. inhabit
   = populate

6. inherent
   = innate
   = inborn

7. inhibit
   = prevent

8. inimical
   = detrimental

9. initiate
   = start

10. innovative
    = novel
    = inventive

11. innuendo
    = overtone
    = hint

12. inquisitive
    = inquiring

13. insinuate
    = allude

14. inspire
    = stimulate
    = motivate

15. integrate
    = combine
    = assimilate

interest〔'ɪntrɪst〕 n. 利益

The *interest* that I earn from the bonds in the banks is the money that I make in addition to my capital. (85 銘傳)

inter	+ est
between	+ exist

inter	+ fere
between	+ strike

interfere〔͵ɪntɚ'fɪr〕 v. 干涉

No foreign country should *interfere* in the internal affairs of our country. (91 彰師大)

interrupt〔͵ɪntə'rʌpt〕 v. 打斷

We were having an interesting conversation when my mother *interrupted* us to say that dinner was ready.

(81 中山)

inter	+ rupt
between	+ break

intonation 〔͵ɪnto'neʃən 〕 *n.* 音調

If one wants to speak English without a
foreign accent, one has to learn correct
intonation. (90 彰師大)

intoxicated 〔 ɪn'tɑksə͵ketɪd 〕 *adj.* 喝醉的

A man who exposes himself when he is
intoxicated, has not the art of getting drunk.

(87 中正)

intrepid 〔 ɪn'trɛpɪd 〕 *adj.* 勇猛的；大膽的

Robert Peary, an *intrepid* explorer, was the
first to reach the North Pole. (90 世新)

intricate 〔'ɪntrəkɪt 〕 *adj.* 錯綜複雜的

Thousands of commuters in major cities
depend upon an *intricate* network of trains.

(87 中正)

in +	tric	+ ate
in +	obstacle +	*v.*

intrigue 〔 ɪn'trig 〕 v. 使感興趣 (= *interest*)

Similarly fascinating coincidences have
intrigued scientists and nonscientists alike
for many years. (87 政大)

introvert 〔 'ɪntrə,vɝt 〕 n. 內向的人

An *introvert* by nature, he preferred reading
a book to going out
with friends. (88 台大)

intro	+	vert
inwards	+	*turn*

invaluable 〔 ɪn'væljəbḷ 〕 adj. 珍貴的

Recent research has provided *invaluable*
information on worldwide weather patterns.

(86 中興)

invest 〔 ɪn'vɛst 〕 v. 投資

She hoped to get rich by *investing* in the
stock market. (83 中興)

investigate 〔 ɪn'vɛstə,get 〕 v. 調查

Scientists are *investigating* ways to extend

human life. (86 逢甲)

```
in + vestigate
 |      |
in +  trace
```

inviolate 〔 ɪn'vaɪəlɪt 〕 adj. 不受侵犯的

Your right to life is *inviolate*; no one can take

it away from you. (89 台大)

invoke 〔 ɪn'vok 〕 v. 求助於

Finally, we *invoke* the power of the law to

prevent a crime. (83 中興)

```
in + voke          in + volve
 |     |             |     |
in + call           in + roll
```

involve 〔 ɪn'vɑlv 〕 v. 包括;牽涉

Could you please be more specific about

what is *involved* in this particular job? (86 台大)

irate 〔aɪ'ret〕 *adj.* 生氣的

The workers were *irate* about the amount of work they were now expected to do. (81 清大)

irresistible 〔͵ɪrɪ'zɪstəbḷ〕 *adj.* 不能抵抗的

If there is an immovable object, there can be no *irresistible* force. (81 政大)

irrespective 〔͵ɪrɪ'spɛktɪv〕 *adj.* 不顧～的

They send information every week, *irrespective* of whether it is useful or not.

(81 政大)

irrevocably 〔ɪ'rɛvəkəblɪ〕 *adv.* 不能挽回地

Machines have changed society *irrevocably*.

(83 清大)

irritable 〔'ɪrətəbḷ〕 *adj.* 性急的

Many people become *irritable* and cannot concentrate after an abnormal event. (90 政大)

irritated ('Irə,tetɪd) *adj.* 疼痛的；發炎的

When we catch a cold, the mucous membrane in the nose becomes *irritated*. (87中正)

isolated ('aɪsḷ,etɪd) *adj.* 孤立的

Weather satellites provide information about weather conditions in *isolated* areas. (85交大)

issue ('ɪʃju) *n.* 議題；關鍵

In foreign language learning, the *issue* at stake is how to motivate the learners. (80逢甲)

J

jaunt (dʒɔnt) *n.* 短程旅行

The Smiths' *jaunt* in the country was very pleasant. (82政大)

jeopardize ('dʒɛpə,daɪz) *v.* 危害

An unresponsive attitude may *jeopardize* the long-term development of the country. (90台大)

Check List

( ) 1. interfere   A. include

( ) 2. intonation   B. touchy

( ) 3. intoxicated   C. drunk

( ) 4. intrepid   D. compelling

( ) 5. intrigue   E. fearless

( ) 6. inviolate   F. regardless

( ) 7. invoke   G. furious

( ) 8. involve   H. intervene

( ) 9. irate   I. outing

( ) 10. irresistible   J. fascinate

( ) 11. irrespective   K. pitch

( ) 12. irrevocably   L. forever

( ) 13. irritable   M. immune

( ) 14. jaunt   N. endanger

( ) 15. jeopardize   O. appeal to

Vocabulary Ratings

5–7 *Good*   8–11 *Very Good*   12–15 *Excellent*

Synonyms

1. interfere
   = intervene

2. irresistible
   = compelling

3. intoxicated
   = drunk

4. intrepid
   = fearless

5. intrigue
   = fascinate

6. irrespective
   = regardless
   = nevertheless

7. invoke
   = appeal to

8. involve
   = include

9. irate
   = furious

10. intonation
    = pitch
    = tone

11. inviolate
    = immune
    = intact

12. irrevocably
    = forever

13. irritable
    = touchy

14. jaunt
    = outing
    = trip

15. jeopardize
    = endanger
    = threaten

jeopardy 〔'dʒɛpədɪ 〕 *n.* 危險

A cut in the budget put 20 percent of the state employee' jobs in *jeopardy*. (85 中興)

juicy 〔'dʒusɪ 〕 *adj.* 有趣的

It is human nature that we love to hear *juicy* stories about other people. (88 銘傳)

juncture 〔'dʒʌŋktʃə 〕 *n.* 時機

At this *juncture* in our nation's affairs, we need firm leadership. (83 中興)

junct + ure
| |
join + *n.*

just + ice
| |
law;*right* + *n.*

justice 〔'dʒʌstɪs 〕 *n.* 司法;正義

The minority groups in this country feel that the *justice* system does not treat them fairly. (91 彰師大)

justification 〔͵dʒʌstəfəˈkeʃən 〕 *n.* 辯護

Many reasons were presented in *justification* of the President's policy. (80 中山)

justly 〔ˈdʒʌstlɪ 〕 *adv.* 恰如其份地

Chia-Yi County is *justly* famous for its beautiful mountains and lakes. (90 中正)

K

ken 〔 kɛn 〕 *n.* 知識；了解

That area is beyond my *ken*. So I'll leave it to the expert. (90 台北)

kick 〔 kɪk 〕 *v.* 戒除

It takes patience to *kick* a bad habit, especially if you have indulged in it for a long time. (82 台大)

L

lamentable ('læməntəbḷ) *adj.* 令人惋惜的

What is *lamentable* is that beauty is the
only form of power that most women are
encouraged to seek. (83淡江)

landmark ('lænd,mɑrk) *n.* 地標

New York City has some famous *landmarks*.

(88交大)

lane (len) *n.* 車道

Because of road construction, traffic is
restricted to one *lane* in each direction.

(85台大)

languid ('læŋgwɪd) *adj.* 精神不振的

The extreme heat made every student in the
classroom quite *languid*. (84中興)

latitude 〔'lætə,tjud 〕 *n.* 緯度

Climate in the United States is affected by *latitude*, elevation, distance from oceans, and prevailing winds.

（82 中興）

lat +	itude
|	|
side +	抽象名詞結尾

leading 〔'lidɪŋ 〕 *adj.* 第一流的

This is indeed a *leading* question if I ever heard one. （84 交大）

legal 〔'ligl 〕 *adj.* 合法的；有關法律的

Mr. Chen owns a company. All his *legal* business is handled by a law firm in Taipei. （91 彰師大）

leg +	al
|	|
law +	*adj.*

legitimate 〔 lɪ'dʒɪtəmɪt 〕 *adj.* 正當的； 合法的

The accident that delayed our bus gave us a *legitimate* reason for being late. （85 逢甲）

lethargic 〔 lɪˈθɑrdʒɪk 〕 *adj.* 遲鈍的；
懶洋洋的 (= *sluggish*)

The administration's *lethargic* response to
the problem made the situation worse.

(88 政大)

level 〔ˈlɛvl̩〕 *adj.* 平坦的

The floor is not *level*, so the chair keeps
rolling across it. (88 銘傳)

liability 〔ˌlaɪəˈbɪlətɪ〕 *n.* 責任

The tobacco industry has been under attack
in the courts over *liability* in smoker's
deaths. (90 市北師)

liable 〔ˈlaɪəbl̩〕 *adj.* 容易～的

Be careful with those fireworks; they are
liable to go off unexpectedly. (90 花師)

lie〔laɪ〕*v.* 位於

His clothing *lay* on the floor until his mother picked it up. (90 世新)

limit〔'lɪmɪt〕*v.* 限制

With his own clinic, the dentist was able to *limit* the number of patients he saw. (90 師大)

loathe〔loð〕*v.* 厭惡

They *loathe* a rowdy crowd. (84 交大)

loophole〔'lup‚hol〕*n.* 漏洞

Some candidates looked for *loopholes* in the law in order to win seats. (84 中興)

lump〔lʌmp〕*n.* 腫塊

He had a *lump* on his head where someone had hit him when he walked home the night before. (91 彰師大)

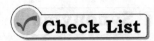

Check List

( ) 1. jeopardy   A. knowledge

( ) 2. juncture   B. sluggish

( ) 3. justification   C. danger

( ) 4. justly   D. lawful

( ) 5. ken   E. quit

( ) 6. kick   F. point

( ) 7. lamentable   G. flat

( ) 8. languid   H. regrettable

( ) 9. legal   I. obligation

( ) 10. lethargic   J. defense

( ) 11. level   K. prone

( ) 12. liability   L. rightly

( ) 13. liable   M. despise

( ) 14. loathe   N. swelling

( ) 15. lump   O. lethargic

Vocabulary Ratings

5–7 *Good*   8–11 *Very Good*   12–15 *Excellent*

Synonyms

1. jeopardy
   = danger

2. juncture
   = point

3. justification
   = defense

4. justly
   = rightly

5. ken
   = knowledge

6. kick
   = quit
   = give up

7. lamentable
   = regrettable

8. languid
   = lethargic

9. legal
   = lawful

10. lethargic
    = sluggish
    = lazy

11. level
    = flat
    = even

12. liability
    = obligation

13. liable
    = prone

14. loathe
    = despise
    = detest

15. lump
    = swelling
    = bump

lung 〔 lʌŋ 〕 *n.* 肺

Smoking causes air pollution and harms our
lungs. (88 銘傳)

M

magnanimous 〔 mæg'nænəməs 〕 *adj.*
寬宏大量的

He was such a *magnanimous* man that he
forgave those people who had insulted
him. (81 師大)

magn + anim + ous
| | |
great + *mind* + *adj.*

magnate 〔 'mægnet 〕 *n.* 大亨

He is a well-known shipping *magnate*,
who owns more than 100 container ships.

(90 政大)

magn +　　　 ate
great + 人的名詞結尾

magnitude〔'mægnə,tjud〕 *n.* 重大；重要

The crisis of liberal education is an
intellectual crisis of the
greatest *magnitude*.

（81 中興）

```
magn + itude
  |       |
great +  n.
```

maintain〔men'ten〕 *v.* 保持

Dennis does not want to gain or lose weight.
He is trying to *maintain* his present weight.

（85 彰師）

major〔'medʒɚ〕 *n.*（陸、空軍）少校

The *major* chatted casually with the reporters
before meeting the press.（90 屏師）

makeshift〔'mek,ʃɪft〕 *adj.* 暫時的

This is a *makeshift* plan until we decide
what to do.（80 政大）

malformed 〔͵mæl'fɔrmd 〕 *adj.* 畸形的

She gave birth to a *malformed* baby. (82 政大)

malign 〔 mə'laɪn 〕 *v.* 誹謗

During the gubernatorial campaign neither
of the two candidates *maligned* the other.

(86 政大)

mali +	gn
|	|
badly +	*produce*

maltreat 〔 mæl'trit 〕 *v.* 虐待

His behavior patterns suggested he had been
badly *maltreated* as a child. (91 世新)

mandatory 〔'mændə͵torɪ 〕 *adj.* 強制性的
(= *compulsory*)

The government has stipulated a *mandatory*
retirement age of 65. (88 政大)

manifest 〔'mænə,fɛst 〕 v. 表示

The teacher *manifested* his disgust with a frown. (90 政大)

mani + fest
| |
hand + strike

mark 〔 mɑrk 〕 v. 標明

Victory celebrations were held to *mark* the end of the war. (90 花師)

markedly 〔'mɑrkɪdlɪ 〕 adv. 顯著地

University tuition varies *markedly* from a few hundred dollars to several thousand.

(86 中興)

merit 〔'mɛrɪt 〕 v. 應得

This petition *merits* more serious attention than it has so far received. (81 清大)

microcosm 〔'maɪkrə,kɑzm̩〕 n. 微觀世界；縮圖

The human body is sometimes seen as a *microcosm* of the universe. (83 台大)

micro	+	cosm
small	+	*universe*

millennium 〔 mɪ'lɛnɪəm〕 n. 一千年

The new *millennium* is certain to be full of new challenges and discoveries. (88 世新)

mille	+ enn	+ ium
thousand	+ *year*	+ *n.*

mimic 〔'mɪmɪk〕 v. 模仿 (= *imitate*)

Some birds can *mimic* human speech. (84 中興)

miniature 〔'mɪnɪətʃɚ〕 adj. 小規模的

A dictionary is just a *miniature* encyclopedia from which we can learn many things. (89 逢甲)

modest 〔'mɑdɪst 〕 *adj.* 謙虛的

When she says that her success is due to good luck, she's being *modest.* (79 師大)

momentum 〔 mo'mɛntəm 〕 *n.* 動力

Commitment and vision form a *momentum* of their own, which brings about a successful conclusion. (83 淡江)

monarch 〔'mɑnək 〕 *n.* 君主

Queen Victoria ruled for almost 64 years--longer than any other British *monarch.*

(82 中興)

```
mon + arch
 |     |
one + chief
```

monologue 〔'mɑnḷ͵ɔg 〕 *n.* 獨白

The audience was very interested in Charles Brown's *monologue.* (82 政大)

Check List

( ) 1. magnanimous   A. deserve

( ) 2. magnate   B. generous

( ) 3. magnitude   C. emperor

( ) 4. makeshift   D. abuse

( ) 5. malformed   E. importance

( ) 6. malign   F. miniature

( ) 7. maltreat   G. imitate

( ) 8. mandatory   H. tycoon

( ) 9. manifest   I. compulsory

( ) 10. markedly   J. deformed

( ) 11. merit   K. humble

( ) 12. microcosm   L. temporary

( ) 13. mimic   M. obviously

( ) 14. modest   N. criticize

( ) 15. monarch   O. reveal

Vocabulary Ratings

5–7 *Good*   8–11 *Very Good*   12–15 *Excellent*

Synonyms

1. magnanimous
   = generous

2. magnate
   = tycoon

3. magnitude
   = importance

4. makeshift
   = temporary

5. malformed
   = deformed

6. malign
   = criticize
   = defame

7. maltreat
   = abuse

8. mandatory
   = compulsory

9. manifest
   = reveal

10. markedly
    = obviously
    = distinctly

11. merit
    = deserve
    = call for

12. microcosm
    = miniature

13. mimic
    = imitate

14. modest
    = humble
    = meek

15. monarch
    = emperor
    = ruler

moonlight 〔'mun,laɪt 〕 v. 兼差

(= *do two jobs*)

He insists on *moonlighting* as a means of
increasing his income. (84 中興)

motivate 〔'motə,vet 〕 v. 引起動機

Japan's recession has *motivated* consumers
to cut back on buying cars. (90 政大)

muddle 〔'mʌdl̩ 〕 v. 胡亂應付 < *through* >

Even though he managed to *muddle* through
the interview, he doesn't think he got the job.

(89 台大)

multilingual 〔,mʌltɪ'lɪŋgwəl 〕 *adj.* 使用多
種語言的

Switzerland is a *multilingual* nation. Its
residents speak French, German, and Italian.

(89 逢甲)

mutual 〔'mjutʃʊəl 〕 *adj.* 互相的

Bob and I have a *mutual* agreement. I water his plants when he goes on vacation, and he does the same for me. (87 逢甲)

myriad 〔'mɪrɪəd 〕 *n.* 無數

The computer programmer worked hard to change a *myriad* of details of the program.

(90 台北)

N

nadir 〔'nedɚ 〕 *n.* 最低點

Economists believe that the *nadir* of the slump has passed and the economy will soon improve.

(90 成大)

name-calling 〔'nem,kɔlɪŋ 〕 *n.* 辱罵

Despite *name-calling* from friends, Steve left a party when kids headed for the bedrooms.

(83 淡江)

natural 〔'nætʃərəl 〕 *adj.* 自然的；天然的

When the first white men came to America, they found vast amounts of *natural* resources.

（90 成大）

negative 〔'nɛgətɪv 〕 *adj.* 負面的；反對的

Janet is a very *negative* person; she often complains about everything. （87 逢甲）

negligent 〔'nɛglədʒənt 〕 *adj.* 疏忽的

The teacher was found guilty of being *negligent* in allowing the children to swim in dangerous water.

（90 政大）

neg +	lig	+ ent
|	|	|
not +	*choose* +	*adj.*

negligible 〔'nɛglɪdʒəbl 〕 *adj.* 微不足道的

Some physicists have proposed that sunspots have *negligible* effects on the earth's weather.

（90 中正）

negotiation 〔 nɪˌgoʃɪˈeʃən 〕 *n.* 談判

The two countries conducted peace *negotiations* to end the war. (91 清大)

neurotic 〔 njuˈratɪk 〕 *adj.* 神經過敏的；非常不安的

People who live on a fixed income have an almost *neurotic* fear of inflation. (90 成大)

niece 〔 nis 〕 *n.* 姪女；外甥女

My sister had a baby daughter yesterday, and she is my first *niece*. (86 台大)

nomination 〔 naməˈneʃən 〕 *n.* 提名

Offer the *nomination* to whoever commands the respect of the people.

(90 世新)

nomin + ation
│   │
name + *n.*

nondescript ('nɑndɪ,skrɪpt) *adj.* 沒有特徵的

A criminal is often a *nondescript* person whom witnesses can never recall clearly.

（82政大）

non +	de +	script
|	|	|
not +	*down* +	*write*

nostalgic (nɑs'tældʒɪk) *adj.* 懷舊的

Listening to Elvis's music makes her feel *nostalgic*. （88世新）

notion ('noʃən) *n.* 概念（ = *idea* ）

Despite *notions* to the contrary, a great deal of technical writing is at best awkward and at worst actually unclear. （88政大）

notoriously (no'torɪəslɪ) *adv.* 惡名昭彰地

The rainfall is *notoriously* variable and unreliable, making it difficult to predict weather conditions. （80逢甲）

novice ('nɑvɪs) *n.* 生手

The *novice* driver was very nervous the first
time he drove his car on
the highway. (91 清大)

nov + ice
| | |
new + 行為者

nuance (nju'ɑns) *n.* (音調、措詞、感情等
的) 細微差異

Body language is not easy to comprehend
because it is full of *nuances*. (81 政大)

nutritional (nju'trɪʃənl̩) *adj.* 有營養的

Fruit and vegetables are an important part
of a *nutritional* diet. (87 逢甲)

O

obliged (ə'blaɪdʒd) *adj.* 有義務的

His boss felt *obliged* to give him a raise in
salary because he had done
such a good job. (87 台大)

ob + lige + d
| | |
to + *bind* + *adj.*

Check List

(   ) 1. moonlight   A. discussion

(   ) 2. muddle (through)   B. communal

(   ) 3. multilingual   C. pessimistic

(   ) 4. mutual   D. careless

(   ) 5. nadir   E. do two jobs

(   ) 6. name-calling   F. bottom

(   ) 7. negative   G. trivial

(   ) 8. negligent   H. manage

(   ) 9. negligible   I. idea

(   ) 10. negotiation   J. insults

(   ) 11. neurotic   K. gradation

(   ) 12. nondescript   L. polyglot

(   ) 13. notion   M. beginner

(   ) 14. novice   N. ordinary

(   ) 15. nuance   O. anxious

Vocabulary Ratings

5–7 *Good*   8–11 *Very Good*   12–15 *Excellent*

Synonyms

1. moonlight
   = do two jobs

2. muddle through
   = manage

3. multilingual
   = polyglot

4. mutual
   = communal

5. nadir
   = bottom

6. name-calling
   = insults
   = abuse

7. negative
   = pessimistic

8. negligent
   = careless

9. negligible
   = trivial

10. negotiation
    = discussion
    = arbitration

11. neurotic
    = anxious
    = irrational

12. nondescript
    = ordinary

13. notion
    = idea

14. novice
    = greenhorn
    = beginner

15. nuance
    = gradation
    = subtlety

observe 〔əb'zɜv〕 *v.* 注意

All human rights must be *observed*. (83淡江)

obstacle 〔'abstəkḷ〕 *n.* 障礙

The computer programmer discovered an
obstacle that had to be overcome. (85交大)

ob	+ sta	+ cle
against	+ stand	+ *n.*

obvious 〔'abvɪəs〕 *adj.* 明顯的

It's *obvious* that there are still some
disadvantages to the plan he presented. (90義守)

occult 〔ə'kʌlt〕 *adj.* 玄奧的；超自然的

During the medieval epoch, the sciences
were considered to be based on the *occult*.

(84政大)

omniscient 〔 ɑm'nɪʃənt 〕 *adj.* 無所不知的

Feeling *omniscient*, people can destroy
themselves by ignoring
possible risks. (83台大)

omni + scient
| |
all + *knowing*

onset 〔'ɑn͵sɛt 〕 *n.* 襲擊；開始 (= *beginning*)

The *onset* of sleep is determined by many
factors. (90中正)

onus 〔'onəs 〕 *n.* 責任；負擔 (= *obligation*)

The *onus* of bringing up six children was on
the father. (90交大)

oppose 〔 ə'poz 〕 *v.* 反對

We shall pay any price and *oppose* any foe
to assure the survival and success of liberty.

(87中興)

op + pose
| |
against + *put*

optical 〔ˋɑptɪk!〕 *adj.* 視覺的

Vermeer was extremely interested in color and the *optical* qualities of light. (82 中興)

optimal 〔ˋɑptəməl〕 *adj.* 最佳的；最適宜的

The *optimal* temperature range for growing mushrooms is from 55°F to 72°F. (87 中興)

optimistic 〔͵ɑptəˋmɪstɪk〕 *adj.* 樂觀的

City residents are *optimistic* that transportation will be improved in the near future. (82 中山)

ordeal 〔ˋɔrdil〕 *n.* 痛苦的經驗

Jennifer Wang was lucky to survive her eight-day kidnap *ordeal*. (86 交大)

organism 〔ˋɔrgən͵ɪzəm〕 *n.* 有機物

Viruses are very small *organisms*. (81 中興)

orthodox 〔ˈɔrθəˌdɑks〕*adj.* 正統的；正當的

Information on individuals should not

be used for other than

orthodox purposes.（82 交大）

ortho	+	dox
|		|
right	+	*opinion*

ostensibly 〔ɑsˈtɛnsəblɪ〕*adv.* 表面上地

He left the country *ostensibly* for medical

treatment, but in fact to avoid prosecution.

（90 政大）

os	+	tens	+	ibly
|		|		|
before	+	*stretch*	+	*adv.*

outcome 〔ˈaʊtˌkʌm〕*n.* 結果

The *outcome* of the experiment was very

encouraging.（90 義守）

outfit 〔ˈaʊtˌfɪt〕*n.* 服裝

The bride planned to buy an entire *outfit* in

red — dress, hat, shoes, and so on.（91 彰師大）

outing (ˈaʊtɪŋ) *n.* 出遊;遠足

To go on an *outing* means to take a short
pleasure trip. (79 師大)

outpace (aʊtˈpes) *v.* 速度比～快

Markets are not perfectly valued at all times,
so the stock market can *outpace* economic
growth. (88 政大)

overbearing (ˌovɚˈbɛrɪŋ) *adj.* 盛氣
凌人的

Robert has become quite *overbearing*. (82 政大)

overcome (ˌovɚˈkʌm) *v.* 克服

Will the ruling party be able to *overcome*
all their immense difficulties?

(86 台大)

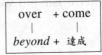

overhaul 〔͵ovɚˈhɔl 〕 *v.* 徹底檢查

Next year we are going to *overhaul* the curriculum. (80 政大)

overlap 〔ˈovɚ͵læp 〕 *v.* 部份重疊

Economics and politics are best studied together as the two subjects *overlap*. (83 淡江)

overlook 〔͵ovɚˈlʊk 〕 *v.* 忽略

The study has either been forgotten or *overlooked*, because no one mentioned it at the meeting. (90 師大)

overwhelmingly 〔͵ovɚˈhwɛlmɪŋlɪ 〕 *adv.* 壓倒性地

The Senate *overwhelmingly* approved an anti-terrorism bill Wednesday. (85 清大)

( ) 1. observe   A. pompous

( ) 2. obstacle   B. visual

( ) 3. occult   C. notice

( ) 4. onset   D. result

( ) 5. onus   E. best

( ) 6. oppose   F. hindrance

( ) 7. optical   G. ignore

( ) 8. optimal   H. torment

( ) 9. ordeal   I. beat

( ) 10. orthodox   J. mysterious

( ) 11. ostensibly   K. traditional

( ) 12. outcome   L. start

( ) 13. overbearing   M. seemingly

( ) 14. overcome   N. burden

( ) 15. overlook   O. disagree

Vocabulary Ratings

5–7 *Good*   8–11 *Very Good*   12–15 *Excellent*

Synonyms

1. observe
   = notice

2. obstacle
   = hindrance

3. occult
   = mysterious

4. onset
   = start

5. onus
   = burden

6. oppose
   = disagree
   = resist

7. optical
   = visual

8. optimal
   = best

9. ordeal
   = torment

10. orthodox
    = traditional
    = standard

11. ostensibly
    = seemingly
    = apparently

12. outcome
    = result

13. overbearing
    = pompous

14. overcome
    = beat
    = defeat

15. overlook
    = ignore
    = neglect

P

palatable 〔'pælətəbḷ〕 *adj.* 美味的 (= *tasty*)

The steak was quite *palatable*. (83 政大)

panacea 〔ˌpænə'siə〕 *n.* 萬靈丹 (= *remedy*)

Many young couples believe that divorce is
a *panacea* for all matrimonial ills. (90 交大)

panic 〔'pænɪk〕 *n.* 恐慌

The outbreak of foot-and-mouth disease in
Taiwan caused a *panic*. (86 中興)

paradoxical 〔ˌpærə'dɑksɪkḷ〕 *adj.* 矛盾的

It is *paradoxical* that Socrates was so
intelligent, so brave, so honorable and so
ugly. (83 淡江)

para	+	dox	+	ical
contrary to	+	opinion	+	adj.

paralyze 〔'pærə,laɪz 〕 v. 使癱瘓

The huge volume of commuter traffic *paralyzes* the city's roads during the rush hours. (91 世新)

parasite 〔'pærə,saɪt 〕 n. 寄生蟲

Currency speculators are considered to be *parasites* on the economy. (88 政大)

parole 〔 pə'rol 〕 n. 假釋

The jury recommended life in prison without the possibility of *parole* for the murderers.

(85 清大)

pass 〔 pæs 〕 v. 傳給

Pass me the suntan lotion before I turn as red as a lobster. (90 市北師)

penalty 〔'pɛnl̩tɪ 〕 n. 處罰

If you cheat on the test, you will suffer a *penalty*. (82 中山)

pen	+ alty
punish +	*n.*

penetrate 〔'pɛnə,tret〕 v. 穿透 (= *pierce*)

The dog's bite slowly *penetrated* my skin.

(83 交大)

perfidious (pɚ'fɪdɪəs) *adj.* 不忠的；奸詐的 (= *treacherous*)

She is a *perfidious* woman who has an
insatiable desire to get
ahead in the world.

(84 淡江)

per	+	fid	+	ious
away	+	trust	+	adj.

permanently 〔'pɝmənəntlɪ〕 *adv.* 永久地

The pizza deliveryman's hearing and
eyesight were *permanently* damaged. (87 政大)

per	+	man	+	ently
through	+	remain	+	adv.

permitted 〔 pɚˈmɪtɪd 〕 *adj.* 被許可的

Slang and substandard language are not generally *permitted* in published scientific papers. (87中興)

perpendicularly 〔ˌpɝpənˈdɪkjələ⋅lɪ 〕 *adv.* 垂直地

The frog's ability to flick its tongue depends on a group of muscles that are arranged *perpendicularly*. (84政大)

per	+	pend	+ i + cul(e) +	ar
|		|	|	|
through	+	*pendent*	+ *n.* +	*adj.*
		下垂的		

perpetual 〔 pɚˈpɛtʃʊəl 〕 *adj.* 永久的；長期的（ = *enduring* ）

Artistic activity demands *perpetual* devotion.

(90市北師)

per	+ pet	+ ual
|	|	|
throughout	+ *seek*	+ *adj.*

persist 〔 pɚˋsɪst 〕 v. 持續

The good weather will *persist* all week.

（83中興）

perspective 〔 pɚˋspɛktɪv 〕 n. 正確的眼光；透徹的看法

Pastor Chen always views things from a religious *perspective*. （81交大）

persuade 〔 pɚˋswed 〕 v. 說服

She *persuaded* her friend to go camping with her. （86台大）

per	+ suade
thorough	+ *advise*

persuasive 〔 pɚˋswesɪv 〕 adj. 有說服力的

His success in persuading people was largely a result of his *persuasive* arguments.

（87淡江）

pertinent ('pɝtn̩ənt) *adj.* 有關的
(= *relevant*)

More powerful computers are needed to
process all the *pertinent* information. (86 中興)

pervade (pɚ'ved) *v.* 充滿；瀰漫

Her work is *pervaded* by nostalgia for a
past age. (91 世新)

per	+ vade
thoroughly +	*go*

petrified ('pɛtrə,faɪd) *adj.* 石化的

The largest *petrified* forest in the world is
in northern Arizona. (90 世新)

petty ('pɛtɪ) *adj.* 瑣碎的 (= *trivial*)

Some employees tend to bother the
supervisor with *petty* matters. (90 台大)

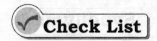

Check List

( ) 1. palatable
( ) 2. panacea
( ) 3. parole
( ) 4. penalty
( ) 5. penetrate

( ) 6. perfidious
( ) 7. permanently
( ) 8. permitted
( ) 9. perpetual
( ) 10. persist

( ) 11. perspective
( ) 12. persuasive
( ) 13. pertinent
( ) 14. petrified
( ) 15. petty

A. convincing
B. pierce
C. trivial
D. treacherous
E. outlook

F. tasty
G. relevant
H. forever
I. endure
J. remedy

K. allowed
L. anxiety
M. fossilized
N. punishment
O. enduring

Vocabulary Ratings

5–7 *Good*   8–11 *Very Good*   12–15 *Excellent*

Synonyms

1. palatable
   = tasty

2. panacea
   = remedy

3. panic
   = anxiety

4. penalty
   = punishment

5. penetrate
   = pierce

6. perfidious
   = treacherous
   = unfaithful

7. permanently
   = forever

8. permitted
   = allowed

9. perpetual
   = enduring

10. persist
    = endure
    = continue

11. perspective
    = outlook
    = standpoint

12. persuasive
    = convincing

13. pertinent
    = relevant

14. petrified
    = fossilized
    = rigidified

15. petty
    = trivial
    = trifling

phase 〔 fez 〕 *n.* 月的盈虧

Some civilizations base their calendar on the *phases* of the moon. (86中興)

phenomenal 〔 fə'nɑmənḷ 〕 *adj.* 驚人的；了不起的

Nancy's ability to skate is *phenomenal.* (83交大)

physical 〔'fɪzɪkḷ 〕 *adj.* 有形的；實物的

The automobile tire tracks are an important piece of *physical* evidence. (90成大)

physiological 〔,fɪzɪə'lɑdʒɪkḷ 〕 *adj.* 生理的

We must have food, water, air, and rest to satisfy our *physiological* needs. (86交大)

piety 〔'paɪətɪ 〕 *n.* 孝順

The Chinese folk story "Ten Brothers" examines the traditional value of filial *piety.*

(89淡江)

pile 〔 paɪl 〕 *v.* 堆積

The child enjoyed *piling* up the wooden bricks then knocking them down. (86 台大)

placate 〔'pleket 〕 *v.* 安慰

The taxi driver offered to pay for the damage in order to *placate* the other driver. (84 交大)

planetarium 〔ˌplænə'tɛrɪəm 〕 *n.* 天文館

They will meet us in front of the *planetarium*.

(83 交大)

plausible 〔'plɔzəbl̩ 〕 *adj.* 似乎合理的

The most *plausible* explanation for the recession is that people have lost confidence in the economy. (88 台大)

pleasing 〔'plizɪŋ 〕 *adj.* 令人喜愛的

The optical properties of a diamond give it the beauty that makes it *pleasing* as a gem.

(86 中興)

pleasurable (ˈplɛʒərəbḷ) *adj.* 令人愉快的

A fortunate but small number of people work at jobs which are in themselves *pleasurable*.

(87 淡江)

plebiscite (ˈplɛbəˌsaɪt) *n.* 公民投票

President Chen declared he would not call a *plebiscite* to solve the sovereignty row with mainland China. (89 逢甲)

pledge (plɛdʒ) *v.* 保證；發誓

The U.S. government *pledged* to supply Taiwan with advanced defensive weapons.

(87 逢甲)

plunge (plʌndʒ) *v.* 投入；衝

The plane exploded in mid-air and *plunged* into the ocean. (86 中興)

pocket ('pɑkɪt) *n.* 一小群;一小批

The country has always had *pockets* of
scarcity in the midst of relative plenty. (台大)

pollution (pə'luʃən) *n.* 污染

Pollution has been a major focus in the green
movement to improve the environment.

(85 銘傳)

ponder ('pɑndɚ) *v.* 沉思

His voice deserves to be heard, his message
pondered. (81 淡江)

portfolio (port'folɪ,o) *n.* 有價證券;畫冊

Portfolio diversity means that one should
invest one's money in various products.

(85 銘傳)

Portfolios have traditionally been used in
art or architecture
classes. (89 文化)

port +	folio
carry +	*a sheet of paper*

postulate 〔'pɑstʃə,let 〕 *v.* 假定

Scientists have recently *postulated* a new theory of how man migrated from Africa to Asia. (90 台大)

potential 〔 pə'tɛnʃəl 〕 *n.* 潛力

A child who cannot concentrate in school may still have excellent *potential* as a student. (86 交大)

potent	+	ial
powerful	+	*n.*

practical 〔'præktɪkl̩ 〕 *adj.* 實際的

Please try to be more *practical*. (84 交大)

precautions 〔 prɪ'kɔʃənz 〕 *n. pl.* 預防措施

We should take all reasonable *precautions* to make sure that the data is reliable. (82 交大)

precision〔prɪˈsɪʒən〕*n.* 精確(= *accuracy*)

The *precision* of tools in the computer manufacturing company has declined.

(86 逢甲)

prediction〔prɪˈdɪkʃən〕*n.* 預測

The *predictions* of rain were so alarming that we canceled the canoe trip. (86 交大)

predilection〔͵prɪdɪˈlɛkʃən〕*n.* 偏好

Learning foreign languages has been my *predilection* since childhood. (89 淡江)

preeminence〔prɪˈɛmənəns〕*n.* 卓越;傑出

The *preeminence* of the newspaper as a daily source of information has been undermined.

(86 逢甲)

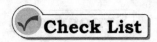
Check List

( ) 1. phenomenal   A. consider
( ) 2. physical   B. assume
( ) 3. placate   C. credible
( ) 4. plausible   D. forecast
( ) 5. pleasure   E. astonishing

( ) 6. plebiscite   F. dive
( ) 7. pledge   G. preference
( ) 8. plunge   H. infection
( ) 9. pollution   I. substantial
( ) 10. ponder   J. accuracy

( ) 11. postulate   K. pleasing
( ) 12. precision   L. soothe
( ) 13. prediction   M. excellence
( ) 14. predilection   N. poll
( ) 15. preeminence   O. promise

Vocabulary Ratings

5–7 *Good*   8–11 *Very Good*   12–15 *Excellent*

Synonyms

1. phenomenal
   = astonishing

2. physical
   = substantial

3. placate
   = soothe

4. plausible
   = credible

5. pleasurable
   = pleasing

6. plebiscite
   = direct vote
   = poll

7. pledge
   = promise

8. plunge
   = dive

9. pollution
   = infection

10. ponder
    = consider
    = muse

11. postulate
    = assume
    = presume

12. precision
    = accuracy

13. prediction
    = forecast

14. predilection
    = preference
    = liking

15. preeminence
    = excellence
    = superiority

preliminary 〔 prɪˈlɪməˌnɛrɪ 〕 *adj.* 初步的

The results of this study are *preliminary* and limited. (86 中興)

premise 〔 ˈprɛmɪs 〕 *n.* 前提 (= *assumption*)

The 28-year-old high school operates on the *premise* that you should teach students values.

(90 市北師)

```
pre  + mise
 |       |
before + send
```

preoccupation 〔 priˌɑkjəˈpeʃən 〕 *n.*
全神貫注

America has a *preoccupation* with physical appearance these days. (83 清大)

prerequisite 〔 ˌpriˈrɛkwəzɪt 〕 *n.* 先決條件

The only *prerequisite* for membership in this club is an IQ of over 150. (87 台大)

prescription 〔 prɪˈskrɪpʃən 〕 *n.* 處方

After examining me, the doctor gave me a *prescription* to be filled at the drugstore.

（80 交大）

preservation 〔 ˌprɛzəˈveʃən 〕 *n.* 保存

Before the invention of refrigeration, the *preservation* of fish and meat was a problem.（90 花師）

press 〔 prɛs 〕 *n.* 新聞界

The politician spoke at a brief *press* conference at the CKS International Airport.（89 淡江）

presume 〔 prɪˈzum 〕 *v.* 假定 (= *assume*)

The Court may *presume* that the choices made by plaintiffs are free and uncoerced.

（85 中興）

pre	+	sume
before	+	*take*

prevalent ('prɛvələnt) *adj.* 普遍的

Where volcanoes are *prevalent*, lakes are created as water collects in volcanic craters. (87 中正)

prevarication (prɪˌværə'keʃən) *n.* 搪塞

Prevarication was natural to John in dealing with the Incas. (82 淡江)

primarily ('praɪˌmɛrəlɪ) *adv.* 主要地

Users of Linux are *primarily* Internet service providers, software developers, universities and, now, large corporations. (90 師大)

prime (praɪm) *n.* 全盛時期 (= *peak*)

Steam engines have now passed the *prime* of their usefulness. (80 淡江)

principal (ˈprɪnsəpḷ) *n.* 本金

The *principal* of the loan is the sum of
money I borrowed. (85 銘傳)

priority (praɪˈɔrətɪ) *n.* 優先權

The badly wounded take *priority* for medical
attention over those only slightly hurt.

(85 逢甲)

privilege (ˈprɪvḷɪdʒ) *n.* 榮幸

It is my *privilege* to speak on behalf of all
the staff members and welcome you to our
country. (81 逢甲)

probation (proˈbeʃən) *n.* 試用 (期)

A new job often has a *probation* period of
three months. (86 中興)

prob + ation
| |
test + *n.*

probe〔 prob 〕 *v.* 探查；探求

Chimpanzees use sticks to *probe* for insects
in narrow spaces.（90台大）

proceedings〔 prə'sidɪŋz 〕 *n. pl.* 訴訟程序

That couple is to divorce and necessary
legal *proceedings* are under way.（85清大）

process〔'prɑsɛs 〕 *v.* 加工；處理

The poppy is *processed* legally into
codeine and morphine.

（89政大）

pro	+ cess
forward +	go

prodigious〔 prə'dɪdʒəs 〕 *adj.* 驚人的

It is extraordinary enough for a first novel,
but is *prodigious* for an author of twenty-two.

（87政大）

produce 〔 prəˈdjus 〕 v. 生產;製造

The fickle behavior of nature both *produces* life and destroys it.

（85 交大）

pro	+ duce
forward	+ *lead*

professional 〔 prəˈfɛʃənḷ 〕 n. 專家

Nowadays *professionals* in certain fields are having difficulty finding jobs. （84 交大）

proficient 〔 prəˈfɪʃənt 〕 adj. 精通的

After studying English intensively for several years, Helen became *proficient*.

（90 輔大）

pro	+ fici	+ ent
forward	+ *make*	+ *adj.*

profundity 〔 prəˈfʌndətɪ 〕 n. 深度

The professor commented that his writing lacked *profundity*. （81 淡江）

Check List

(   ) 1. preliminary   A. chiefly

(   ) 2. premise   B. peak

(   ) 3. preoccupation   C. assumption

(   ) 4. prerequisite   D. procedure

(   ) 5. press   E. explore

(   ) 6. prevalent   F. requirement

(   ) 7. prevarication   G. initial

(   ) 8. primarily   H. amazing

(   ) 9. prime   I. equivocation

(   ) 10. principal   J. fixation

(   ) 11. probation   K. widespread

(   ) 12. probe   L. expert

(   ) 13. proceeding   M. media

(   ) 14. prodigious   N. test

(   ) 15. proficient   O. capital

Vocabulary Ratings

5–7 *Good*   8–11 *Very Good*   12–15 *Excellent*

Synonyms

1. preliminary
   = initial

2. premise
   = assumption

3. preoccupation
   = fixation

4. prerequisite
   = requirement

5. press
   = media

6. prevalent
   = widespread
   = prevailing

7. prevarication
   = equivocation

8. primarily
   = chiefly

9. prime
   = peak

10. principal
    = capital
    = funds

11. probation
    = trial
    = test

12. probe
    = explore

13. proceeding
    = procedure

14. prodigious
    = amazing
    = wonderful

15. proficient
    = expert
    = skilled

proliferate ﹝ prə'lɪfə,ret ﹞ v. 急速增加

As attendance at museums and galleries increases, new exhibition facilities *proliferate*.

（90 成大）

pro	+	li	+	fer	+	ate
forward	+	nourish	+	bear	+	v.

proliferation ﹝ pro,lɪfə'reʃən ﹞ n. 激增

The increase in sexual freedom for women was probably due to the *proliferation* of contraceptive devices. （83 淡江）

prologue ﹝'prolog﹞ n. 序言；開場白

This novel is famous for its *prologue*. （82 政大）

pro	+ logue
before	+ speech

pro	+ mote
forward	+ move

promote ﹝ prə'mot ﹞ v. 升遷

I hear that the company plans on *promoting* him soon because of his good work. （85 逢甲）

promulgate 〔 prəˈmʌlget 〕 v. 公布

As soon as the board of elections
promulgates the list of candidates, a secret
vote is prepared.

（85 中興）

pro + mulg + ate
| | |
before + *people* + *v.*

prone 〔 pron 〕 *adj.* 容易的

Tom is *prone* to illness due to malnutrition.

（89 東華）

proof 〔 pruf 〕 *n.* 證據 (= *evidence*)

The scientist needed more *proof* before his
theory could be accepted. （87 中正）

propagate 〔ˈprɑpəˌget 〕 v. 傳播

Rumors have been *propagated* all over the
country that a meteor will collide with the
earth. （90 台大）

property 〔'prɑpətɪ〕 *n.* 特性

Many *properties* of the atmosphere affect the amount of solar radiation that reaches the earth. (86 中興)

proportion 〔 prə'porʃən 〕 *n.* 比例

Are you paid in *proportion* to the number of hours you work? (83 中興)

propose 〔 prə'poz 〕 *v.* 提議

At the conclusion of the meal the host rose and *proposed* a toast. (台大)

pro + pose	pro + secut + ion
forward + put	*forth + follow + n.*

prosecution 〔 ˌprɑsɪ'kjuʃən 〕 *n.* 起訴

In all criminal *prosecutions* a man has a right to know the cause and nature of his accusation. (81 中興)

proximity 〔 prɑk'sɪmətɪ 〕 *n.* 鄰近

The *proximity* of raw material attracted many
manufacturers. (90 義守)

punctual 〔 'pʌŋktʃʊəl 〕 *adj.* 準時的

Being *punctual* for a job interview is
important. (87 逢甲)

purchaser 〔 'pɝtʃəsɚ 〕 *n.* 顧客

That shop provides *purchasers* with a
one-year guarantee on this washing machine.

(90 屏師)

pursue 〔 pɚ'su 〕 *v.* 追捕；追求

Officer Smith *pursued* the criminal for
many years. (81 清大)

pur + sue
| |
forth + follow

Q

qualifying 〔ˈkwɑləˌfaɪɪŋ〕 *adj.* 資格檢定的

I am very busy working hard for my Ph. D
qualifying exams. (84 交大)

qualms 〔 kwɔmz 〕 *n. pl.* 不安

Peter had no *qualms* about borrowing money
from his friends. (82 政大)

quarantine 〔ˈkwɔrənˌtin〕 *v.* 檢疫

No passengers on the ship are allowed to
leave without being *quarantined* first. (84 中興)

R

rampant 〔ˈræmpənt〕 *adj.* 猖獗的；蔓延的
(= *unchecked*)

Malaria is still *rampant* in some swampy
regions. (83 政大)

randomly （ˈrændəmlɪ ）*adv.* 隨機地；
不加選擇地（ = *indiscriminately* ）

The people interviewed for the survey were
randomly selected. (90 中正)

ransom （ˈrænsəm ）*n.* 贖金

Kidnappers often demand money, which is
called a *ransom*. (88 逢甲)

rapport （ ræˈport ）*n.* 密切的關係

The best salespeople try to build *rapport*
with the customers before they try to sell
them anything. (81 政大)

rational （ˈræʃənḷ ）*adj.* 有理性的

My math teacher is *rational*; she always
follows a logical method. (86 交大)

rat	+ ion	+ al
reason +	n. +	adj.

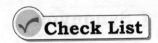

Check List

( ) 1. proliferate

( ) 2. prologue

( ) 3. promulgate

( ) 4. prone

( ) 5. propagate

( ) 6. proportion

( ) 7. propose

( ) 8. prosecution

( ) 9. proximity

( ) 10. pursue

( ) 11. qualms

( ) 12. rampant

( ) 13. randomly

( ) 14. rapport

( ) 15. rational

A. offer

B. chase

C. by chance

D. preface

E. trial

F. liable

G. uncertainty

H. mushroom

I. connection

J. spread

K. sensible

L. ratio

M. publicize

N. unchecked

O. closeness

Vocabulary Ratings

5–7 *Good*   8–11 *Very Good*   12–15 *Excellent*

Synonyms

1. proliferate
   = mushroom

2. prologue
   = preface

3. promulgate
   = publicize

4. prone
   = liable

5. propagate
   = spread

6. proportion
   = ratio
   = share

7. propose
   = offer

8. prosecution
   = trial

9. proximity
   = closeness

10. pursue
    = chase
    = track

11. qualms
    = anxiety
    = uncertainty

12. rampant
    = unchecked

13. randomly
    = by chance

14. rapport
    = connection
    = bond

15. rational
    = sensible
    = logical

rationalization 〔͵ræʃən̩lɪˈzeʃən 〕 *n.* 合理化

Many people offer a *rationalization* for poor
behavior that is really just an excuse. (90台大)

rebuttal 〔 rɪˈbʌtəl 〕 *n.* 反駁

Mayor Chen made a *rebuttal* to what they
said in the meeting. (84交大)

recent 〔ˈrisn̩t 〕 *adj.* 最近的

When I applied for my passport to be
renewed, I had to send a *recent* photograph.

(86台大)

recluse 〔 rɪˈklus 〕 *n.* 隱士

He refused to see anyone and remained a
recluse to the end of his life. (87淡江)

recognition 〔͵rɛkəgˈnɪʃən 〕 *n.* 認可；承認

The actor wanted public *recognition*. (86交大)

recognize 〔'rɛkəg,naɪz〕 v. 認出

Peter had changed so much that I hardly *recognized* him. (81 中山)

reconcile 〔'rɛkən,saɪl〕 v. 和解

It is unlikely that their dispute will be *reconciled*. (89 東華)

```
re  + concile
|        |
again + 使和諧
```

```
re   + cruit
|        |
again + grow
```

recruit 〔rɪ'krut〕 v. 招募（新成員）

The Red Lions, Taipei's premier soccer team, is now *recruiting* new players. (89 淡江)

recycle 〔ri'saɪkḷ〕 v. 回收

The *recycling* of aluminum conserves ninety-five percent of the energy needed to make new metal. (89 逢甲)

reduction 〔 rɪ'dʌkʃən 〕 *n.* 減少

The figures show a *reduction* in the number
of unemployed people
in Taipei. (86 台大)

re	+ duct +	ion
back +	*lead* +	*n.*

redundant 〔 rɪ'dʌndənt 〕 *adj.* 多餘的;
重複的

Repetition of words and ideas may make
your speech *redundant*. (90 成大)

reform 〔 rɪ'fɔrm 〕 *v.* 改革

The governor hopes to *reform* the old
university scholarship program. (89 逢甲)

regard 〔 rɪ'gɑrd 〕 *n.* 關係
(*with regard to* 關於~)

With *regard* to your summer house, would
you rent it to us next year? (87 台大)

regenerate 〔 rɪˈdʒɛnəret 〕 *v.* 革新；使更生

The northern humanists proposed to *regenerate* mankind within the framework of the existing political and religious order.

（80 中興）

regressive 〔 rɪˈgrɛsɪv 〕 *adj.* 退化的

The patient's behavior is *regressive*.

（86 政大）

re	+ gress	+ ive
back +	*go* +	*adj.*

rehabilitate 〔 riəˈbɪlə,tet 〕 *v.* 使恢復

Do you think the mental institution will really *rehabilitate* my friend George? （84 交大）

reiterate 〔 riˈɪtə,ret 〕 *v.* 重複

Even as many of them *reiterate* their pledges of support, their actions believe their words.

（90 成大）

re	+ iterate
again +	*repeat*

rejoice 〔 rɪ'dʒɔɪs 〕 v. 高興

Everyone *rejoiced* at the news of his safe return. (85 中興)

rejuvenate 〔 rɪ'dʒuvə,net 〕 v. 使返老還童；使恢復活力

"Use of our beauty cream will *rejuvenate* your skin," the advertisement claimed.

(87 淡江)

re	+ juven +	ate
again +	*young* +	*v.*

relationship 〔 rɪ'leʃən,ʃɪp 〕 n. 關係

The birth of twins was considered an unnatural *relationship* in some cultures.

(85 交大)

relative 〔 'rɛlətɪv 〕 n. 親戚

You can choose your friends, but you can't choose your *relatives*. (83 中興)

relatively 〔ˈrɛlətɪvlɪ 〕*adv.* 相對地

For a college student, sports are *relatively* unimportant when compared with studying.

（88 逢甲）

reliable 〔 rɪˈlaɪəbl̩ 〕*adj.* 可信賴的

（ = *dependable* ）

Many employers have discovered that elderly persons are very *reliable* workers. （84 中正）

reluctant 〔 rɪˈlʌktənt 〕*adj.* 不情願的

Although Sam had seen the accident, he was *reluctant* to act as a witness. （80 中正）

re	+ luct	+ ant
back	+ struggle	+ adj.

re	+ medy
again	+ heal

remedy 〔ˈrɛmədɪ 〕*n.* 補救方法 （ = *cure* ）

The only *remedy* for your poor pronunciation is to practice over and over again. （87 中正）

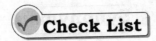
Check List

( ) 1. rebuttal	A. renew
( ) 2. recognize	B. sign up
( ) 3. reconcile	C. going back
( ) 4. recruit	D. delight
( ) 5. recycle	E. refutation
( ) 6. reduction	F. reuse
( ) 7. redundant	G. revive
( ) 8. regenerate	H. surplus
( ) 9. regressive	I. identify
( ) 10. rehabilitate	J. restore
( ) 11. reiterate	K. kin
( ) 12. rejoice	L. settle
( ) 13. rejuvenate	M. repeat
( ) 14. relative	N. unwilling
( ) 15. reluctant	O. decrease

Vocabulary Ratings

5–7 *Good*   8–11 *Very Good*   12–15 *Excellent*

Synonyms

1. rebuttal
   = refutation

2. recognize
   = identify

3. reconcile
   = settle

4. recruit
   = sign up

5. recycle
   = reuse

6. reduction
   = decrease
   = drop

7. redundant
   = surplus

8. regenerate
   = renew

9. regressive
   = going back

10. rehabilitate
    = restore
    = recover

11. reiterate
    = repeat
    = do again

12. rejoice
    = delight

13. rejuvenate
    = revive

14. relative
    = kin
    = relation

15. reluctant
    = unwilling
    = hesitant

remote 〔 rɪ'mot 〕 *adj.* 偏遠的

Seeking peace and clean air, many young people have moved from cities to *remote* areas of the country. (80逢甲)

render 〔'rɛndɚ 〕 *v.* 使成為

Pollution has *rendered* the soil unfit for vegetation. (89台大)

ren + der	re + patri + ate
| |	| | |
back + give	*out + father + v.*

repatriate 〔 ri'petrɪ,et 〕 *v.* 遣返

The government decided to *repatriate* those foreign workers because they had no visas.
(90政大)

replete 〔 rɪ'plit 〕 *adj.* 充滿的 (= *filled*)

Our language is *replete* with clichés that have their origins in Freud's writings. (82淡江)

replica ('rɛplɪkə) *n.* 複製品

The old man owns a statue of Socrates that is a *replica*, or copy, of a statue in Athens, Greece. (80 逢甲)

report (rɪ'port) *v.* 報導

The newspaper *reported* that seven persons had been drowned. (90 成大)

reprimand (ˌrɛprə'mænd) *v.* 懲戒

The students were *reprimanded* for being too noisy. (85 清大)

reproof (rɪ'pruf) *n.* 譴責

One can scarcely expect to escape *reproof* for such irresponsible behavior. (83 台大)

reputation (ˌrɛpjə'teʃən) *n.* 聲譽

He has an excellent *reputation* as a criminal lawyer. (85 台大)

rescue 〔'rɛskju 〕 v. 解救

It was too late to *rescue* the animal. (81 淡江)

resent 〔 rɪ'zɛnt 〕 v. 痛恨

Many people fear and *resent* immigration.

(90 台北)

 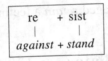

resist 〔 rɪ'zɪst 〕 v. 抗拒

I couldn't *resist* another slice of cake even though I was supposed to be on a diet.

(86 台大)

resources 〔 rɪ'sorsɪz 〕 n. pl. 資源

The ocean provides the island people rich *resources* for living. (81 交大)

restriction 〔 rɪˈstrɪkʃən 〕 *n.* 限制

Some states have *restrictions* on how many terms a politician may serve. (86 交大)

retain 〔 rɪˈten 〕 *v.* 保留

Because of their importance to the community, the aged *retain* a feeling of self worth.

(83 淡江)

retaliate 〔 rɪˈtælɪˌet 〕 *v.* 報復 (= *revenge*)

The discontented students *retaliated* by boycotting the school cafeteria. (84 淡江)

re	+ tali	+ ate
back	+ talion	+ v.

re	+ tard
back	+ slow

retard 〔 rɪˈtɑrd 〕 *v.* 減緩;延遲 (= *postpone*)

The only thing that *retards* aging is calorie restriction. (90 市北師)

retentive 〔 rɪ'tɛntɪv 〕 *adj.* 記性好的

Peter has a *retentive* mind; he remembers almost everything he sees or hears. (84台大)

retire 〔 rɪ'taɪr 〕 *v.* 退休

It had been a long day, so I *retired* early.

(91世新)

retrograde 〔 'rɛtrə,gred 〕 *adj.* 退步的

This is a *retrograde* development. (82政大)

retrospect 〔 'rɛtrə,spɛkt 〕 *n.* 回顧

In *retrospect* I see that the problems I encountered last month were really minor.

(86政大)

reunion 〔 rɪ'junjən 〕 *n.* 團聚

We had a family *reunion* where I saw relatives I hadn't seen for 10 years. (91世新)

review 〔 rɪ'vju 〕 *v.* 復習

She spent the summer *reviewing* Taiwanese history as she was to teach that in the fall.

（82 台大）

revoke 〔 rɪ'vok 〕 *v.* 撤回

The class has *revoked* their original decision to have a field trip.

（91 世新）

re	+ voke
|	|
back	+ *call*

revolt 〔 rɪ'volt 〕 *n.* 叛亂

A prisoner threw herself from the roof of a six-story jail during a prison *revolt* here last night. （91 清大）

revolutionize 〔 ˌrɛvə'luʃənˌaɪz 〕 *v.* 革新

The invention of the computer has *revolutionized* people's lives. （88 交大）

Check List

( ) 1. remote   A. hate

( ) 2. repatriate   B. revenge

( ) 3. replete   C. copy

( ) 4. replica   D. review

( ) 5. reprimand   E. punishment

( ) 6. reproof   F. cancel

( ) 7. reputation   G. distant

( ) 8. resent   H. blame

( ) 9. retaliate   I. rebellion

( ) 10. retard   J. send home

( ) 11. retrograde   K. postpone

( ) 12. retrospect   L. fame

( ) 13. review   M. backward

( ) 14. revoke   N. filled

( ) 15. revolt   O. go over

Vocabulary Ratings

5–7 *Good*   8–11 *Very Good*   12–15 *Excellent*

Synonyms

1. remote
   = distant

2. repatriate
   = send home

3. replete
   = filled

4. replica
   = copy

5. reprimand
   = punishment

6. reproof
   = blame
   = criticism

7. reputation
   = fame

8. resent
   = hate

9. retaliate
   = revenge

10. retard
    = postpone
    = delay

11. retrograde
    = backward
    = declining

12. retrospect
    = review

13. review
    = go over

14. revoke
    = cancel
    = withdraw

15. revolt
    = rebellion
    = uprising

rise〔 raɪz 〕 *v.* 上升

People demand higher wages all the time because prices are always *rising*. (86 台大)

room 〔 rum 〕 *n.* 機會；空間

There's always *room* for improvement however much you've already done. (90 花師)

rudimentary 〔 ˌrudə'mɛntərɪ 〕 *adj.* 基本的 (= *fundamental*)

Computer programs can teach *rudimentary* concepts such as shapes, colors, numbers and letters. (90 市北師)

rumble 〔 'rʌmbḷ 〕 *v.* (雷聲、車輛、肚子等) 轆轆或隆隆作響

His stomach was already *rumbling* for lunch.

(80 政大)

rummage 〔'rʌmɪdʒ〕 v. 翻找

The student *rummaged* through her locker looking for her chemistry assignment. (89 台大)

rustic 〔'rʌstɪk〕 adj. 鄉村的；粗野的

Those who live in cities think country folks have *rustic* manners.

(87 淡江)

rus(t)	+	ic
country+		adj.

ruthlessly 〔'ruθlɪslɪ〕 adv. 無情地；殘酷地

In the book, the vices and follies of some of the characters make them behave *ruthlessly*.

(88 政大)

S

sacrilegious 〔͵sækrɪ'lɪdʒəs〕 adj. 該受天譴的

Many themes considered *sacrilegious* in the nineteenth century are treated casually today.

(90 世新)

salubrious (sə'lubrɪəs) *adj.* 有益健康的

(= *healthy*)

Their marriage is not a *salubrious* one. It
will culminate in a debacle. (84 淡江)

salvage ('sælvɪdʒ) *v.* 搶救

Our task is to decide what equipment can be
salvaged. (90 政大)

sanction ('sæŋkʃən) *n.* 制裁

One of the *sanctions* was a ban on
international investment. (81 逢甲)

sanct	+	ion
sacred	+	n.

sangu	+	ine
blood	+	adj.

sanguine ('sæŋgwɪn) *adj.* 樂觀的

Doctors suggest that the best prescription for
success against cancer might be a *sanguine*
personality. (84 中興)

sardonic 〔sɑr'dɑnɪk〕*adj.* 嘲弄的；挖苦的

Intellectuals have a tendency to be *sardonic*.

(84 交大)

savvy 〔'sævɪ〕*adj.* 聰明的

Bill Gates' success is due to his *savvy* business decisions. (89 淡江)

say 〔se〕*n.* 發言權

Being a member of this club, I believe I have a *say* in this matter. (91 彰師大)

scatter 〔'skætə〕*v.* 散布

Garbage is *scattered* all along the highway because there is no fine for littering. (81 中山)

scribble 〔'skrɪbḷ〕*v.* 潦草書寫

Mary forgot to take a notebook to class, so she had to *scribble* her notes on the back of an envelope.

(86 政大)

scrib(b) + le
| |
scribe + *v.*

script 〔 skrɪpt 〕 *n.* （戲劇廣播的）腳本

Having read the *script* of the play, the producer began to think how he would cast it. （90花師）

scrupulously 〔'skrupjələslɪ 〕 *adv.* 小心地

To avoid contamination, surgeons wash their hands *scrupulously* before starting each operation. （84政大）

scrutinize 〔'skrutə,naɪz 〕 *v.* 詳細審查

All the applicants for the job are thoroughly *scrutinized* for their suitability. （85台大）

scuffle 〔'skʌfḷ 〕 *n.* 扭打

Several brief *scuffles* at voting stations in Taipei were reported. （89淡江）

season 〔'sizṇ 〕 *n.* 季節

Peaches are in *season* now and can be bought at any supermarket. （81師大）

secluded (sɪˈkludɪd) *adj.* 偏僻的

For centuries, little was known about Antarctica, the most *secluded* continent.

(88 政大)

se	+ clude	+ d
apart	+ shut	+ adj.

secretly (ˈsikrɪtlɪ) *adv.* 秘密地

He sometimes looks on the sly. The phrase "on the sly" means *secretly*. (87 淡江)

seemingly (ˈsimɪŋlɪ) *adv.* 表面上；看起來

A labyrinth is a confusing and *seemingly* endless array of passages. (89 東華)

segregation (ˌsɛgrɪˈgeʃən) *n.* 種族隔離

Martin Luther King was a great hero who fought against *segregation*. (81 交大)

se	+ gregat	+ ion
apart	+ collect	+ n.

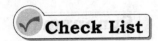
Check List

( ) 1. rudimentary   A. scrawl

( ) 2. rummage   B. remote

( ) 3. rustic   C. mercilessly

( ) 4. ruthlessly   D. sarcastic

( ) 5. sacrilegious   E. clever

( ) 6. salubrious   F. impious

( ) 7. salvage   G. carefully

( ) 8. sanguine   H. basic

( ) 9. sardonic   I. examine

( ) 10. savvy   J. dig

( ) 11. scribble   K. rescue

( ) 12. scrupulously   L. fight

( ) 13. scrutinize   M. rural

( ) 14. scuffle   N. positive

( ) 15. secluded   O. healthy

Vocabulary Ratings

5–7 *Good*   8–11 *Very Good*   12–15 *Excellent*

Synonyms

1. rudimentary
   = basic

2. rummage
   = dig

3. scrupulously
   = carefully

4. ruthlessly
   = mercilessly

5. sacrilegious
   = impious

6. salubrious
   = healthy
   = wholesome

7. salvage
   = rescue

8. sanguine
   = positive

9. sardonic
   = sarcastic

10. savvy
    = clever
    = shrewd

11. scribble
    = scrabble
    = scrawl

12. rustic
    = rural

13. scrutinize
    = examine

14. scuffle
    = fight
    = wrestle

15. secluded
    = isolated
    = remote

seize 〔 siz 〕 *v.* 扣押；沒收 (= *confiscate*)

The Taichung Port Authority has *seized*
over a million dollars. (85 中興)

self-annihilation 〔 ˈsɛlfəˌnaɪəˈleʃən 〕 *n.*
自我毀滅

Few impulses have been as persistent as the
drive toward *self-annihilation*. (90 政大)

```
an  +  nihil    + ation
 |        |         |
to  +  nothing  +   n.
```

senior 〔 ˈsinjɚ 〕 *adj.* 年長的 (= *elderly*)

Senior citizens who qualify for assistance
can receive monthly allowances. (90 市北師)

sentimental 〔 ˌsɛntəˈmɛntl̩ 〕 *adj.* 感情的；
情緒的 (= *emotional*)

Conscience is merely a *sentimental* reaction
after too much love or wine. (87 中正)

sequence ('sikwəns) *n.* 順序

A computer will always follow the same *sequence* when solving a problem. (86 中興)

sequ	+ ence
follow	+ *n.*

shameful ('ʃɛmfəl) *adj.* 可恥的

Ms. Lin always tells her students that it's not *shameful* to ask questions in class. (90 師大)

shatter ('ʃætə) *v.* 使粉碎

Peter *shattered* the living room window with one of his golf balls. (86 政大)

shortcut ('ʃɔrt,kʌt) *n.* 捷徑

Genetic engineering provides a dramatic *shortcut* by transplanting new genes. (82 台大)

siblings 〔'sɪblɪŋz 〕 *n. pl.* 兄弟姊妹

Disrespect to parents or *siblings* shouldn't be part of any loving home. (83 淡江)

simulation 〔,sɪmjə'leʃən 〕 *n.* 模仿

Many games are *simulations* that attempt to model some real-life situation. (89 文化)

simultaneously 〔,saɪml̩'tenɪəslɪ 〕 *adv.*
同時地 (= *at the same time*)

It is possible for people to carry on several on-line conversations *simultaneously*. (87 中正)

simul + taneous + ly
| | |
same + *adj.* + *adv.*

singe 〔 sɪndʒ 〕 *v.* 燒焦

The hair of several firemen was slightly *singed* when they attempted to put out the fire. (90 花師)

skeptical 〔'skɛptɪkl̩〕 *adj.* 懷疑的

I'm *skeptical* of the team's chances of winning. (83 清大)

skillful 〔'skɪlfəl〕 *adj.* 巧妙的；熟練的

People have to be patient and *skillful* when they deal with those around them. (90 師大)

slash 〔slæʃ〕 *v.* 大幅削減 (= *cut*)

In times of economic difficulty, budgets for research and development are often *slashed* first. (84 政大)

slender 〔'slɛndɚ〕 *adj.* 苗條的

The *slender* thief was able to enter the apartment through the narrow window. (82 淡江)

sluggish 〔'slʌgɪʃ〕 *adj.* 遲緩的；懶洋洋的

Hot weather makes me *sluggish*. (80 政大)

solitude ('salə,tjud) *n.* 孤獨

Sometimes one wants to be with people,
and sometimes one
needs *solitude*. (90台大)

soli + tude
| |
sole + *n*

solution (sə'luʃən) *n.* 解決之道

Successful problem solving requires finding
the right *solution* to the right problem. (86中興)

somewhat ('sʌm,hwɑt) *adv.* 有一點

"The survival of the fittest" is a *somewhat*
misleading phrase. (91清大)

sophisticated (sə'fɪstɪ,ketɪd) *adj.* 複雜的

Chimpanzees in the wild use simple objects
as tools, but in laboratory situations they can
use more *sophisticated* items. (91清大)

soph +	ist +	ic +	ate +	d
|	|	|	|	|
wise +	*person* +	*adj.* +	*v.* +	*adj.*

sovereign 〔'savrɪn 〕 *adj.* 主權獨立的

Only *sovereign* states are able to make treaties. (80 淡江)

span 〔 spæn 〕 *n.* (持續) 時間

Children may be difficult to teach because of their short attention *span*. (85 台大)

spark 〔 spark 〕 *v.* 引起

The recent interest rate rises have *sparked* new problems for the government. (90 政大)

spectator 〔'spɛktetɚ 〕 *n.* 觀眾

Too much TV watching tends to cause children to be passive *spectators*. (90 輔大)

spect	+ at(e) +	or
see	+ *v.* +	*person*

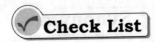
Check List

( ) 1. seize   A. trigger

( ) 2. sentimental   B. all together

( ) 3. sequence   C. duration

( ) 4. simulation   D. free

( ) 5. simultaneously   E. confiscate

( ) 6. singe   F. emotional

( ) 7. skeptical   G. inactive

( ) 8. slash   H. order

( ) 9. sluggish   I. audience

( ) 10. solitude   J. burn

( ) 11. somewhat   K. cut

( ) 12. sovereign   L. seclusion

( ) 13. span   M. imitation

( ) 14. spark   N. rather

( ) 15. spectator   O. doubtful

Vocabulary Ratings

5–7 *Good*   8–11 *Very Good*   12–15 *Excellent*

Synonyms

1. seize
   = confiscate

2. sentimental
   = emotional

3. sequence
   = order

4. simulation
   = imitation

5. simultaneously
   = all together

6. singe
   = burn
   = flame

7. skeptical
   = doubtful

8. slash
   = cut

9. sluggish
   = inactive

10. solitude
    = seclusion
    = isolation

11. somewhat
    = rather
    = fairly

12. sovereign
    = free

13. span
    = duration

14. spark
    = activate
    = trigger

15. spectator
    = audience
    = viewer

speculate ('spɛkjə,let) v. 沉思

He *speculates* on the wisdom of asking for a raise. (89 東華)

spice (spaɪs) v. 加以香料

Ketchup was developed from a tasty, *spiced* Chinese sauce. (90 世新)

split (splɪt) v. 分配;分擔

The dealer wanted to sell the camera for $4000 and I wanted to pay $3000, so we finally agreed to *split* the difference. (85 台大)

stamina ('stæmənə) n. 活力 (= *strength*)

Most students will muster up all their *stamina* to prepare for the final examination.

(79 政大)

stammer ('stæmɚ) n. 口吃

He has a nervous *stammer*. (91 清大)

standoff 〔'stænd,ɔf 〕 *n.* 僵持

Police surrounded the building and the *standoff* lasted three days. (85 清大)

staple 〔'stepḷ 〕 *v.* (用釘書針) 釘

I think you'd better *staple* these sheets of paper together before they get separated.

(90 花師)

status 〔'stetəs 〕 *n.* 地位

Clothing may indicate a person's social *status*. (81 交大)

staunchly 〔'stɑʊntʃlɪ 〕 *adv.* 堅定地

One man arose from the crowd and *staunchly* accepted the challenge. (83 交大)

stereotype 〔'stɛrɪə,taɪp 〕 *n.* 刻板印象

The *stereotype* of Americans is that they drive big cars, drink beer, and eat hot dogs. (81 交大)

stern〔 stɜn 〕 *adj.* 嚴格的（= *strict*）

Many people are beginning to call for *sterner* measures. (83 政大)

stigmatize〔'stɪgmə,taɪz 〕 *v.* 指責；
打上烙印

People with criminal records are *stigmatized* by society. (90 台大)

stipulate〔'stɪpjə,let 〕 *v.* 規定

The law *stipulates* every car must have seat belts for the driver and every passenger. (90 政大)

store〔 stor 〕 *v.* 儲存（= *keep*）

The potatoes were *stored* in the warehouse.
(80 中正)

strained〔 strend 〕 *adj.* 緊張的

The Beijing-Taipei-Washington triangle is becoming *strained*. (90 台北)

strait 〔 stret 〕 *n.* 海峽

The Foundation for Exchanges across the Taiwan *Strait* is an intermediary agency.

(80 交大)

strenuously 〔'strɛnjʊənslɪ 〕 *adv.* 激烈地

It is not true that you need protein when exercise *strenuously*. (81 政大)

stressful 〔'strɛsfəl 〕 *adj.* 有壓力的

Steve has a very *stressful* job; he needs a vacation. (88 逢甲)

strictly 〔'strɪktlɪ 〕 *adv.* 嚴格地

She wasn't, *strictly* speaking, beautiful in the accepted sense but she was very attractive.

(90 花師)

strike 〔 straɪk 〕 *v.* 達成

They are conscious of the difficulty of *striking* a balance between soap opera and dignity. (台大)

striking ('straɪkɪŋ) *adj.* 顯著的

The most *striking* technological success has been the computer revolution. (86 中興)

struggle ('strʌgl̩) *n.* 奮鬥

Much of the music that Verdi wrote is associated with the *struggle* for the unification of Italy. (82 中興)

subject (səb'dʒɛkt) *adj.* 易受～的

If a country is not strong, her overseas citizens are often *subject* to ill treatment.

(89 淡江)

subordinate (sə'bɔrdn̩ɪt) *v.* 使成為次要；使居下位

Mary *subordinated* her own interests to those of John by letting him have the scholarship.

(88 台大)

sub	+ ordin	+ ate
under	+ order	+ v.

subsidize ﹝'sʌbsəˌdaɪz﹞ *v.* 資助

In every western country the State *subsidizes* education, housing and health provision.

（85 中興）

substitute ﹝'sʌbstəˌtjut﹞ *n.* 代替品

Detergent is a soap *substitute* used for washing and cleaning. （86 中興）

sub	+ stitute
|	|
in place of	+ *place*

suc	+ cinct
|	|
under	+ *bind*

succinct ﹝səkˈsɪŋkt﹞ *adj.* 簡潔的

You should delete this paragraph in order to make your essay more *succinct.* （88 台大）

suffice ﹝səˈfaɪs﹞ *v.* 足夠

A covering letter should never exceed one page; often a far shorter letter will *suffice.* （87 台大）

suf	+ fice
|	|
under	+ *make*

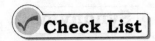

Check List

( ) 1. speculate
( ) 2. stamina
( ) 3. stammer
( ) 4. standoff
( ) 5. staunchly

( ) 6. stern
( ) 7. stigmatize
( ) 8. stipulate
( ) 9. store
( ) 10. strained

( ) 11. strait
( ) 12. strike
( ) 13. subsidize
( ) 14. succinct
( ) 15. suffice

A. channel
B. slur
C. reach
D. deadlock
E. tense

F. firmly
G. demand
H. reflect (on) .
I. finance
J. strict

K. strength
L. concise
M. stutter
N. serve
O. put away

Vocabulary Ratings

5–7 *Good*   8–11 *Very Good*   12–15 *Excellent*

Synonyms

1. speculate
   = reflect (on)

2. stamina
   = strength

3. stammer
   = stutter

4. standoff
   = deadlock

5. staunchly
   = firmly

6. stern
   = strict
   = harsh

7. stigmatize
   = slur

8. stipulate
   = demand

9. store
   = put away

10. strained
    = tense
    = nervous

11. strait
    = canal
    = channel

12. strike
    = reach

13. subsidize
    = finance

14. succinct
    = concise
    = brief

15. suffice
    = serve
    = do

sufficient〔 səˈfɪʃənt 〕 *adj.* 足夠的

Although it hasn't rained for a long time the
newspapers say there will be *sufficient* water
for the summer.（90 輔大）

suggest〔 səˈdʒɛst 〕 *v.* 暗示（ = *insinuate* ）

She didn't say much, but her tone of voice
suggested more.（84 淡江）

summon〔 ˈsʌmən 〕 *v.* 傳喚

He was *summoned* to appear in traffic court.

（88 東華）

supersede〔 ˌsupɚˈsid 〕 *v.* 取代

Now that coal has been *superseded* by
electricity we have much cleaner air.

（84 台大）

super	+	sede
above	+	sit

supersonic 〔͵supɚ'sɑnɪk 〕 *adj.* 超音速的

One of the environmental effects of *supersonic* travel is the sonic boom. (86 中興)

super	+ son	+ ic
|	|	|
over	+ *sound*	+ *adj.*

supple 〔'sʌpḷ 〕 *adj.* 柔軟的；靈活的

(= *limber*)

Dancers exercise regularly, so they have *supple* bodies. (84 中興)

supplement 〔'sʌplə͵mɛnt 〕 *v.* 補充

Martha took a part-time job on weekends in order to *supplement* her income. (85 彰師)

survive 〔 sɚ'vaɪv 〕 *v.* 生存

In prehistoric times, people *survived* by hunting and gathering food. (84 中山)

sur	+ vive
|	|
over	+ *live*

susceptible 〔 sə'sɛptəbḷ 〕 *adj.* 易受影響的

People working under stress are more *susceptible* to health problems. (81 交大)

sus + cept + ible	sus + pen + se
| | |	| | |
under + take + adj.	*under + hang + n.*

suspense 〔 sə'spɛns 〕 *n.* 焦慮；不安

After applying for the job, he was kept in *suspense* for two weeks. (80 逢甲)

swarm 〔 swɔrm 〕 *n.* (昆蟲) 群

There is a *swarm* of flies on the table.

(87 淡江)

sweep 〔 swip 〕 *v.* 橫掃

Rumors of his stepping down from office *swept* the building. (80 政大)

synchronize 〔'sɪŋkrə͵naɪz〕 v. 對（鐘錶的）時間

We had to start at exactly the same time, so we had our watches *synchronized*. （87 淡江）

syndrome 〔'sɪn͵drom〕 n. 症候群

The acquired immune deficiency *syndrome* （AIDS）is likely to strike those whose immune system is weak. （87 台大）

synthesis 〔'sɪnθəsɪs〕 n. 結合體；合成

It really is more accurate to think of knowledge as a *synthesis* of East and West. （90 師大）

syn	+ thesis
|	|
together	+ *putting*

syn	+ thet	+ ically
|	|	|
together	+ *put*	+ *adv.*

synthetically 〔sɪn'θɛtɪkḷɪ〕 adv. 人造地；合成地（= *artificially*）

Scientists are now able to produce more raw materials *synthetically*. （86 中興）

T

tantamount ('tæntə,maʊnt) *adj.* 相等的

John's penalty is *tantamount* to his crime.

(84 交大)

technique (tɛk'nik) *n.* 技術;技巧

This *technique* may be usable in your
business if you can adapt it to your
particular situation. (90 世新)

tedious ('tidɪəs) *adj.* 沉悶的

Rob abhors games that seem *tedious* and
calls them "mindless marathons." (84 政大)

tempo ('tɛmpo) *n.* 節奏 (= *rhythm*)

John did not enjoy the rock concert because
he thought the *tempo* was bad. (90 台大)

temporal 〔'tɛmpərəl 〕 *adj.* 世俗的

They both had the same mission: the spiritual
and *temporal* reorganization of European
society. (8 中興)

temporary 〔'tɛmpə,rɛrɪ 〕 *adj.* 暫時的

Television caused a *temporary* drop in
movie attendance. (85 交大)

temptation 〔 tɛmp'teʃən 〕 *n.* 誘惑

You need to learn to resist the *temptation* to
buy things that are on sale. (81 逢甲)

tenacity 〔 tɪ'næsətɪ 〕 *n.* 固執；不屈不撓

The history of China reveals the *tenacity*
with which the Chinese cling to established
customs. (90 花師)

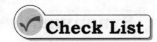
Check List

( ) 1. suggest   A. mixture

( ) 2. summon   B. worldly

( ) 3. supersede C. lure

( ) 4. supple   D. insinuate

( ) 5. susceptible E. equal

( ) 6. synchronize F. limber

( ) 7. synthesis   G. passing

( ) 8. tantamount H. coordinate

( ) 9. technique   I. call for

( ) 10. tedious   J. skill

( ) 11. tempo   K. sensitive

( ) 12. temporal   L. firmness

( ) 13. temporary   M. replace

( ) 14. temptation N. rhythm

( ) 15. tenacity   O. boring

Vocabulary Ratings

5–7 *Good* 8–11 *Very Good* 12–15 *Excellent*

Synonyms

1. suggest
   = insinuate

2. summon
   = call for

3. supersede
   = replace

4. supple
   = limber

5. susceptible
   = sensitive

6. synchronize
   = coordinate
   = match

7. synthesis
   = mixture

8. tantamount
   = equal

9. technique
   = skill

10. tedious
    = boring
    = dull

11. tempo
    = rhythm
    = beat

12. temporal
    = worldly

13. temporary
    = passing

14. temptation
    = lure
    = invitation

15. tenacity
    = resolve
    = firmness

theory 〔'θɪərɪ〕 *n.* 理論

Seldom has the mathematical *theory* of
games been of practical use in playing real
games. (90 屏師)

therapeutic 〔,θɛrə'pjutɪk 〕 *adj.* 治療的

Aspirin is not *therapeutic*, but it does ease
pain in various parts of the body. (90 台大)

therapist 〔'θɛrəpɪst 〕 *n.* 治療專家

John went to a *therapist* for help with his
psychological problems. (81 交大)

thermometer 〔 θə'mɑmətə 〕 *n.* 溫度計

The nurse took the patient's temperature
with a *thermometer*.

(81 師大)

thermo	+	meter
under	+	*bind*

thorough 〔'θɝo 〕 *adj.* 徹底的

The doctor gave the patient a *thorough* examination to discover the cause of his illness. (86 台大)

thoughtful 〔'θɔtfəl 〕 *adj.* 體貼的

Nancy is a very *thoughtful* person. She always thinks of the needs of her friends.

(91 彰師大)

thrifty 〔'θrɪftɪ 〕 *adj.* 節儉的

By spending as little as possible, the *thrifty* old woman was able to live on the little money she had. (79 師大)

thrive 〔 θraɪv 〕 *v.* 繁榮

Taiwan has to take some steps in order to *thrive* in the knowledge-based world economy. (90 輔大)

thrust (θrʌst) *n.* 強加

Some achieve greatness and some have greatness *thrust* upon them. (台大)

tier (tɪr) *n.* 層 (= *layer*)

An avalanche occurs when uneven *tiers* of various snow types are placed under stress.

(80 淡江)

timid (ˈtɪmɪd) *adj.* 膽小的

The *timid* youngster was afraid to ask for a second helping of pie. (79 師大)

topple (ˈtɑpḷ) *v.* 推倒

Typhoon Herb, with winds up to 196 kilometers per hour, *toppled* trees and flooded roads. (86 中興)

toxic (ˈtɑksɪk) *adj.* 有毒的

Arsenic is a *toxic* drug. (81 中興)

transaction 〔 træns'ækʃən 〕 *n.* 交易

It is easy to complete a *transaction* at
the automatic teller
machine. (90 台大)

tran	+ sact	+ ion
across	+ cut	+ *n.*

transition 〔 træn'zɪʃən 〕 *n.* 轉換；轉移

For many reasons, the *transition* from war to
peace is extremely difficult. (81 中興)

transplant 〔 træns'plænt 〕 *v.* 移植

The plants should be grown indoors until
spring, when they can be *transplanted*
outside. (91 世新)

trans	+ plant
across	+ plant

treacherous 〔'trɛtʃərəs 〕 *adj.* 奸詐的；
狡猾的

The *treacherous* little boy stole the old
woman's purse. (84 交大)

tremor 〔'trɛmɚ〕 *n.* 震動 (= *vibration*)

Before the earthquake hit the area, many minor *tremors* were felt. (90中正)

trendy 〔'trɛndɪ〕 *adj.* 時髦的
(= *fashionable*)

Coloring one's hair has become *trendy* recently. (86中興)

trespass 〔'trɛspəs〕 *n.* (對他人權利的) 侵害；非法侵入

The city objected to the government's *trespass* into its educational policies. (84台大)

tres	+ pass
across	+ *pass*

trifling 〔'traɪflɪŋ〕 *adj.* 微不足道的

Don't bother yourself with such *trifling* details; just look for the main ideas of the chapter. (89台大)

trigger 〔'trɪgɚ〕 *v.* 引起 (= *spark*)

Price increases *trigger* demands for wage increases. (83 政大)

turmoil 〔'tɜmɔɪl〕 *n.* 混亂;騷動

The close election led to the political *turmoil*.

(90 台北)

turn 〔tɜn〕 *v.* 變成

Sometimes things don't *turn* out the way we think they are going to. (87 台大)

U

ultimate 〔'ʌltəmɪt〕 *adj.* 最終的

So far the results of the experiment are encouraging, but the *ultimate* outcome is still in doubt. (81 清大)

ultim + ate
| |
last + *adj.*

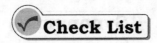
Check List

( ) 1. therapeutic	A. intrusion
( ) 2. thorough	B. in
( ) 3. thrifty	C. push
( ) 4. thrust	D. shake
( ) 5. tier	E. layer
( ) 6. topple	F. deal
( ) 7. toxic	G. complete
( ) 8. transaction	H. petty
( ) 9. transplant	I. frugal
( ) 10. treacherous	J. chaos
( ) 11. tremor	K. healing
( ) 12. trendy	L. transfer
( ) 13. trespass	M. poisonous
( ) 14. trifling	N. sly
( ) 15. turmoil	O. bring down

Vocabulary Ratings

5–7 *Good*   8–11 *Very Good*   12–15 *Excellent*

Synonyms

1. therapeutic
   = healing

2. thorough
   = complete

3. thrifty
   = frugal

4. thrust
   = push

5. tier
   = layer

6. topple
   = bring down
   = knock down

7. toxic
   = poisonous

8. transaction
   = deal

9. transplant
   = transfer

10. treacherous
    = sly
    = crafty

11. tremor
    = vibration
    = shake

12. trendy
    = in

13. trespass
    = intrusion

14. trifling
    = trivial
    = petty

15. turmoil
    = chaos
    = disorder

unanimous 〔 juˈnænəməs 〕 *adj.* 全體一致的

Both churchgoers and non-churchgoers are *unanimous* on the desirability of religious instruction. (90 市北師)

unconscious 〔 ʌnˈkɑnʃəs 〕 *adj.* 無意識的

He looks as if he were *unconscious*. (84 交大)

un	+ con	+ sci	+ ous
|	|	|	|
not	+ *with*	+ *know*	+ *adj.*

uncouth 〔 ʌnˈkuθ 〕 *adj.* 粗野的

It is *uncouth* of the young man to eat with his fingers. (84 交大)

undercover 〔 ˌʌndəˈkʌvə 〕 *adv.* 暗中；秘密地

Because the policeman was working *undercover*, the robbers didn't recognize him. (88 逢甲)

undermine〔͵ʌndə'maɪn〕v. 暗中破壞；
逐漸損害

They offered the player a bribe but could
not *undermine* his integrity. (87 淡江)

undue〔ʌn'dju〕adj. 過度的 (= *excessive*)

The prince thought that his mother had
remarried with *undue* haste. (79 政大)

ungovernable〔ʌn'gʌvənəbḷ〕adj.
無法控制的

He has an *ungovernable* temper; that is,
he is easily irritated. (86 政大)

uniformity〔͵junə'fɔrmətɪ〕n. 一致

Given the existence of so many factions in
the field, it is unrealistic to expect any
uniformity. (90 屏師)

unilateral 〔͵junɪˈlætərəl〕*adj.* 單方面的

Unilateral decisions are made by only one

of the parties concerned.

（90 台大）

uni + later + al
|　　|　　|
one + side + adj.

uninhabitable 〔͵ʌnɪnˈhæbətəbḷ〕*adj.*

不適合居住的

The land has become *uninhabitable*.

People are no longer able to live there.（88 逢甲）

unique 〔juˈnik〕*adj.* 獨一無二的

That's a *unique* idea.（81 淡江）

universal 〔͵junəˈvɝsḷ〕*adj.* 普遍的

Children are children wherever you go.

The curiosity of children is truly *universal*.

（86 中興）

unquestionably 〔 ʌn'kwɛstʃənəblɪ 〕 *adv.*
無疑地；確定地

Unquestionably, there is an element of truth in their observations. (85 台大)

unsympathetic 〔 ˌʌnsɪmpə'θɛtɪk 〕 *adj.*
無情的

A callous person is one who is *unsympathetic*.

(87 淡江)

uprising 〔 'ʌpˌraɪzɪŋ 〕 *n.* 叛變；暴動

The government feared there would be an *uprising* over its taxation policies. (81 清大)

urgent 〔 'ɝdʒənt 〕 *adj.* 緊急的

When he heard the *urgent* call for help, he did not hesitate. (82 淡江)

V

validity 〔vəˈlɪdətɪ〕 *n.* 有效性

Although the proposals are very different, both of them have some *validity*. (89文化)

val + id + ity	van + ish
strong + adj.+ n.	empty + v.

vanish 〔ˈvænɪʃ〕 *v.* 消失

With a wave of his hand, the magician made the rabbit *vanish*. (90義守)

vary 〔ˈvɛrɪ〕 *v.* 不同

Students *vary* in their tastes. (84交大)

vast 〔væst〕 *adj.* 廣大的 (= *enormous*)

The *vast* region was irrigated by the large river and its many tributaries. (90中正)

velocity 〔 vəˈlɑsətɪ 〕 *n.* 速度 (= *speed*)

Mercury's *velocity* is so great that it completes four revolutions around the sun in one year. (88 政大)

vengeance 〔ˈvɛndʒəns 〕 *n.* 報仇；報復

The man promised that he would not seek *vengeance* against the person who had robbed him. (90 台大)

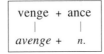

venge + ance	venti + late
avenge + *n.*	*wind* + *bring*

ventilate 〔ˈvɛntəˌlet 〕 *v.* 使通風

The laboratory should be *ventilated* after the experiment is completed. (84 交大)

verdict 〔ˈvɝdɪkt 〕 *n.* 判決

The prosecuting attorney demanded a "guilty" *verdict*. (81 逢甲)

Check List

( ) 1. unanimous		A. speed
( ) 2. unconscious		B. revenge
( ) 3. uncouth		C. excessive
( ) 4. undermine		D. judgment
( ) 5. undue		E. consistency
( ) 6. uniformity		F. united
( ) 7. unilateral		G. freshen
( ) 8. uprising		H. rebellion
( ) 9. urgent		I. unaware
( ) 10. vanish		J. pressing
( ) 11. vary		K. rude
( ) 12. velocity		L. disappear
( ) 13. vengeance		M. one-sided
( ) 14. ventilate		N. differ
( ) 15. verdict		O. damage

Vocabulary Ratings

5–7 *Good* 8–11 *Very Good* 12–15 *Excellent*

Synonyms

1. unanimous
   = united

2. unconscious
   = unaware

3. uncouth
   = rude

4. undermine
   = damage

5. undue
   = excessive

6. uniformity
   = consistency
   = sameness

7. unilateral
   = one-sided

8. uprising
   = rebellion

9. urgent
   = pressing

10. vanish
    = disappear
    = fade away

11. vary
    = differ
    = diverge

12. velocity
    = speed

13. vengeance
    = revenge

14. ventilate
    = air
    = freshen

15. verdict
    = judgment
    = decision

versatile 〔'vɝsətḷ 〕 *adj.* 多才多藝的

In order to repair barns, grow crops, and care for animals, a farmer must indeed be *versatile*.

（90 政大）

versatility 〔ˌvɝsə'tɪlətɪ 〕 *n.* 多用途

A study of the English language reveals a dramatic history and astonishing *versatility*.

（81 交大）

vertigo 〔'vɝtɪˌgo 〕 *n.* 暈眩（ = *dizziness* ）

Problems related to the circulation of blood to the brain or ear can cause *vertigo* in older people. （90 中正）

veteran 〔'vɛtərən 〕 *adj.* 老練的

Young basketball players can learn a lot from *veteran* players. （90 彰師大）

vicarious 〔 vaɪˈkɛrɪəs 〕 *adj.* 感同身受的

The children enjoyed a *vicarious* sense of
power through the exploits of the comic
book hero. (89 東華)

vicinity 〔 vəˈsɪnətɪ 〕 *n.* 附近

The watchman mounted the tower to see if
there were any people in the *vicinity*. (82 淡江)

vigilant 〔ˈvɪdʒələnt 〕 *adj.* 警戒的

The guards ought to be *vigilant* at
all times. (79 政大)

vigil	+	ant
awake	+	adj.

virtually 〔ˈvɜtʃʊəlɪ 〕 *adv.* 實際上

(= *practically*)

The lunch is *virtually* ready. I only have
to finish the vegetables. (83 政大)

virus 〔'vaɪrəs 〕 *n.* 病毒

There are all kinds of *viruses* affecting computers all over the world. (88 銘傳)

visible 〔'vɪzəbḷ 〕 *adj.* 看得見的

X-rays are able to make *visible* details that are otherwise impossible to observe. (91 清大)

```
vis + ible
 |     |
see + adj.
```

vogue 〔 vog 〕 *n.* 時尚；流行

There seems to be a *vogue* for Chinese food at present. (83 淡江)

volcano 〔 vɑl'keno 〕 *n.* 火山

Volcanoes are divided into three main groups.

(90 屏師)

volunteer 〔,vɑlən'tɪr 〕 *adj.* 自願的

Nowadays, many people devote themselves to *voluntèer* work; that is, work without pay.

(80 交大)

voodoo 〔'vudu〕 *n.* 巫毒教

In *voodoo* economics, the economist uses a vague or questionable formula. (85 銘傳)

vouch 〔 vautʃ 〕 *v.* 擔保

I'll be glad to *vouch* for you if you want to open a checking account at my bank.

(86 政大)

vow 〔 vau 〕 *v.* 發誓

Peter *vowed* not to take another drink as long as he lived. (88 東華)

vulnerable 〔'vʌlnərəbḷ 〕 *adj.* 易受傷害的

The general sent all the soldiers out on maneuvers, leaving the fort *vulnerable* to attack. (87 台大)

W

warrant 〔'wɔrənt 〕 v. 證明～爲正當；
表示～爲合理

What she did was wrong, but I don't think it
warranted quite such severe punishment.

（90 政大）

watch 〔 watʃ 〕 n. 警戒

The customs officers were on the *watch* for
someone trying to smuggle illicit goods. （90 花師）

weather 〔'wɛðɚ 〕 v. 平安度過（困境）

Despite the worldwide economic downturn,
many companies were able to *weather* the
recession. （90 政大）

welfare 〔'wɛl,fɛr 〕 n. 福利

Welfare programs for the elderly provide
senior citizens with nursing
homes and regular financial
help. （86 逢甲）

wel	+	fare
good	+	go

wheel 〔hwil〕 *n.* (汽車的) 方向盤;輪子

He was a timid man in most ways but at the *wheel* of his car he was a devil. (90 花師)

widely 〔'waɪdlɪ〕 *adv.* 廣泛地

(= *extensively*)

One of the most *widely* discussed environmental effects of supersonic travel is the sonic boom. (86 中興)

widespread 〔'waɪd'sprɛd〕 *adj.* 普遍的;廣泛的 (= *general*)

The *widespread* use of poisonous chemical fertilizers has declined. (86 逢甲)

will 〔wɪl〕 *n.* 意志力;決心

(= *determination*)

His *will* is stronger than mine. (80 中正)

Check List

( ) 1. versatile		A. locality
( ) 2. vertigo		B. well-being
( ) 3. veteran		C. watchful
( ) 4. vicarious		D. spirit
( ) 5. vicinty		E. empathetic
( ) 6. vigilant		F. trend
( ) 7. virtually		G. all-around
( ) 8. vogue		H. support
( ) 9. vouch		I. broadly
( )10. watch		J. dizziness
( )11. weather		K. survive
( )12. welfare		L. guard
( )13. widely		M. experienced
( )14. widespread		N. general
( )15. will		O. practically

Synonyms

1. versatile
= all-around

2. vertigo
= dizziness

3. veteran
= experienced

4. vicarious
= empathetic

5. vicinity
= locality

6. vigilant
= watchful
= alert

7. virtually
= practically

8. vogue
= trend

9. vouch
= support

10. watch
= guard
= lookout

11. weather
= survive
= outlive

12. welfare
= well-being

13. widely
= broadly

14. widespread
= general
= common

15. will
= guts
= spirit

windfall ('wɪnd,fɔl) *n.* 意外之財

In Taiwan, the stock market is very popular.
People dream of making a *windfall*
overnight. (88 銘傳)

withstand (wɪθ'stænd) *v.* 抵抗

Palm trees produce seeds capable of
withstanding prolonged immersion in salt
water, so palms are found on many
continents. (86 中興)

with	+	stand
against	+	*bear*

wretched ('rɛtʃɪd) *adj.* 悲慘的

He was very unhappy; he led a *wretched*
life. (81 師大)

Z

zany 〔'zenɪ〕 *adj.* 稀奇古怪的；滑稽可笑的

The author is best known for his *zany*
science fiction stories. (81 清大)

zenith 〔'zinɪθ〕 *n.* 頂點；巔峰

The mathematician was working at the *zenith*
of her powers. (84 政大)

全國最完整的文法書 ☆☆☆

文法寶典

劉 毅 編著

這是一套想學好英文的人必備的工具書,作者積多年豐富的教學經驗,針對大家所不了解和最容易犯錯的地方,編寫成一套完整的文法書。

本書編排方式與衆不同,首先給讀者整體的概念,再詳述文法中的細節部分,內容十分完整。文法說明以圖表為中心,一目了然,並且務求深入淺出。無論您在考試中或其他書中所遇到的任何不了解的問題,或是您感到最煩惱的文法問題,查閱文法寶典均可迎刃而解。例如:哪些副詞可修飾名詞或代名詞?(P.228);什麼是介副詞?(P.543);那些名詞可以當副詞用?(P.100);倒裝句(P.629)、省略句(P.644)等特殊構句,為什麼倒裝?為什麼省略?原來的句子是什麼樣子?在文法寶典裏都有詳盡的說明。

例如,有人學了觀念錯誤的「假設法現在式」的公式,

> If + 現在式動詞⋯⋯,主詞 + shall(will, may, can)+ 原形動詞

只會造:If it rains, I will stay at home.

而不敢造:If you *are* right, I *am* wrong.

　　　　 If I *said* that, I *was* mistaken.

　　　(If 子句不一定用在假設法,也可表示條件子句的直說法。)

可見如果學了文法不求徹底了解,反而成為學習英文的絆腳石,對於這些易出錯的地方,我們都特別加以說明(詳見 P.356)。

文法寶典每冊均附有練習,只要讀完本書、做完練習,您必定信心十足,大幅提高對英文的興趣與實力。

● 全套五冊,售價900元。市面不售,請直接向本公司購買。

||||||||||||||||| ● 學習出版公司門市部 ● |||||||||||||||||

台北地區：台北市許昌街 10 號 2 樓　TEL：(02)2331-4060・2331-9209

台中地區：台中市綠川東街 32 號 8 樓 23 室　TEL：(04)2223-2838

|||||||||||||||||||||||||||||||||||||||||||||||||||||||||||||||||||||||||

研究所必考 1000 字

主　　　編 / 林 憶 予

發　行　所 / 學習出版有限公司　　☎ (02) 2704-5525

郵 撥 帳 號 / 0512727-2 學習出版社帳戶

登　記　證 / 局版台業 2179 號

印　刷　所 / 裕強彩色印刷有限公司

台 北 門 市 / 台北市許昌街 10 號 2 F

　　　　　　☎ (02) 2331-4060・2331-9209

台 中 門 市 / 台中市綠川東街 32 號 8 F 23 室 ☎ (04) 2223-2838

台灣總經銷 / 紅螞蟻圖書有限公司　　☎ (02) 2795-3656

美國總經銷 / Evergreen Book Store　☎ (818) 2813622

本公司網址　www.learnbook.com.tw

電 子 郵 件　learnbook@learnbook.com.tw

┌─────────────────────────┐
│　售價：新台幣二百二十元正　│
└─────────────────────────┘

2003 年 6 月 1 日一版二刷

ISBN 957-519-680-5